Fruit

FOR

Tomorrow

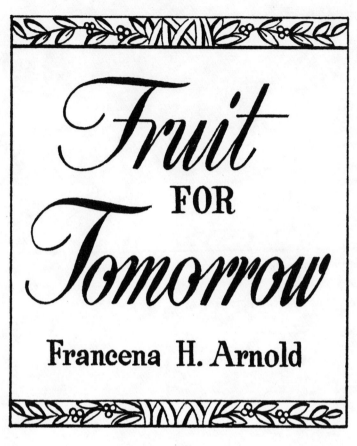

Fruit
FOR
Tomorrow

Francena H. Arnold

ZONDERVAN PUBLISHING HOUSE
GRAND RAPIDS, MICHIGAN

FRUIT FOR TOMORROW
Copyright 1949 by Zondervan Publishing House
Grand Rapids, Michigan

Library of Congress Catalog Card Number: 71-81053

First printing of paperback edition — 1969

Printed in the United States of America

DEDICATED

to

MY CHRISTIAN FOREBEARS

*who loved and served God in such a way
that they brought forth fruit
and their fruit remains.*

Fruit
FOR
Tomorrow

Chapter One

The morning mail was late and Virginia sat on the step waiting for it. She could see the old postman in the next block, so it did not seem worth her while to go into the house and start the ironing she had promised Mrs. Malone she would do before lunch. It was pleasant sitting here on the cool terrace with the shade of the elm tree by the walk protecting her from the heat of the August sun.

Kurt had cut the lawn this morning and the scent of the mown grass brought a hazy memory of childhood days on Grandpa's farm where the perfume of newly-mown hay had hung over the field where she and Jim and Allie May had romped. The soft gurgle of the water trickling from the hose that Kurt had left lying by the young tree which needed special care changed to the music of creek water trickling over stones. The clatter of the lawn mower in the back yard where Kurt was now working became the noise of the big mower in Grandpa's meadow.

The heat of the day was intense, and as Virginia waited she closed her eyes against the glare of the sun on the cars that were scuttling past on the boulevard. The sights and sounds about her faded away, and she heard only the clack of the mower in the big hayfield and the shrill laughter of three children as they tumbled on the haycocks.

A passing car gave a raucous blast of its horn, and she sat up with a start, surprised to find herself here on the terrace of her home on Monterey Boulevard, rather than on the farm.

5

"Whatever made me dream of that?" she asked herself in astonishment. "Why, I haven't thought of the farm or Grandpa or Allie May for years!"

The postman was across the street now, but he would probably sit down on the Ashby's porch and do some sorting while Mr. Ashby got a cool drink for him, so Virginia would have to wait as patiently as she could for the letter from Mexico that she hoped was in his bag. Perhaps she should have started that ironing instead of sitting here dreaming of days and people that were gone out of her life forever. At that thought her brow clouded. Even now, after all the years, it was hard to think that she would never see Grandpa or Allie May again. Of course she would see them in heaven, but today heaven seemed too far away and unreal to be comforting. It was *now* that she wanted to see them.

How strange that anyone so alive and vigorous as Grandpa had been, even during that last summer, should suddenly be gone, and how cruel that the world should go on as if he had never lived. No—not as if he had never lived; for there was Daddy, and Jim, herself, Kurt and Kit. And somewhere—she wished she knew where—Allie May was carrying on, too. Wherever she was, Allie May would have in her more of the life and character of Grandpa than any of them, for she had been with him every day of the first ten years of her life. It had been a family joke that she even tried to walk like him. Virginia remembered hearing a neighbor, laughing at the tall man and the tiny girl, say, "Joe Martin'll never die as long as that youngun lives!"

But Grandpa was gone and no one knew where Allie May was. Even the place where they had lived had been almost forgotten by those who should have remembered. It was a solemn thought that a man could live and labor for almost ninety years, as Grandpa had, and then pass from the earth and leave nothing behind except the few people who bore his name but were so busy with their own lives that they had no time even for memories of him. Would that be the way with all of them who were so full of vigor now? Would the time come when there would be nothing left on earth to show that Virginia Martin had lived? She didn't want it to be that way. She wanted to live in such a way that after she had gone there would be something left to go on living in her stead—something fine and noble that would remain in the hearts and lives of those whom she had touched on her journey.

The postman's step on the walk roused her, and she ran to meet him. The first letter on the stack he handed her was from Mother, and she went around the house to the back yard to read it with Kurt before taking it upstairs to Kit. After Kit got hold of one of Mother's letters no one else had much chance at it. Even Jim, when he came home at night, was allowed to keep it only long enough to read it once.

"O. K., Kittikin, here's your letter," he would say, tossing it back on the bed. "Hold it tight and don't let the goblins get it!"

Kit would make a face at him. "Go ahead and tease! I don't care. It's a letter from my mother!" She would hold the precious missive in her hot, nervous little hands as if by hugging it she could get closer to the mother who had written it.

Virginia and Kurt read this one together, Kurt leaning over her shoulder as she scanned the pages.

"Same old story." he grunted. "Dad's a little better and she's getting along fine. She's a brick, isn't she, Ginny? Never a gripe in the whole time she's been gone. I'll bet it's no fun at all sitting there by Dad's bed when he doesn't even know her. You'd think he'd be coming out of it by this time, wouldn't you?"

His boyish voice was anxious and Virginia hastened to reassure him.

"Mr. Hudson said the doctor said he was doing fine. It takes a long time after such a severe shock. Probably he's lots better even now. This was written over a week ago. It takes so long for mail to get down to the railroad, and even longer for it to reach an airfield, that we can't expect to keep up to date."

"Yep. That's one thing I keep thinking. If he's improving at all, he's always lots better than we hear in these week-old letters. Wouldn't it be super if they got home by the time school starts?"

"Yes—but I don't think they will. Mr. Hudson says Dad will have to gain a lot of strength before he can stand the trip down that mountain. It was just a miracle that they could get him to that little missionary hospital. I'm going to send some of my missionary money down there from now on. No, Kurt, I don't think he'll be able to come before October. Let's hope for his birthday—that's the tenth."

Virginia gathered up the rest of the letters and went back into the house. As she started up the stairs, Kit heard her coming and called,

"Has the mail come, Ginny? Is there a letter from Mother?"

"Yes, indeedy! And it's a big fat one! Here, catch!"

As she came in the door she tossed the letter to the eager hands and said, "You're a big girl, Kitty. You read your letter and I'll read mine."

She sat down in Mother's little rocker by the window and began to sort the other pieces of mail the postman had left. None of it had looked interesting at her first hasty glance— several magazines, some advertisements of lawn seed and house paint, an insurance notice for Jim and a flat, uninteresting envelope for herself. Probably a beauty-parlor ad, or a plea for aid from some organization of which she had never heard. She unfolded it and read the few short lines it contained, her eyes opening in astonishment and her cheeks flushing with excitement. She read it again, and felt herself go weak with the realization of its meaning. It just *couldn't* be!

Virginia glanced at Kit who was laboring over Mother's letter and had not noticed her agitation. Dumping the rest of the mail into the rocker, she sped down the hall to her own room with the letter that had caused so much agitation.

There, with the door closed against any intrusion, she read and reread the missive until the words were photographed in her mind and her brain accepted the wonderful fact disclosed there. Miss Curtis had resigned, and she—Virginia Martin—had been chosen to fill the position vacated. That bare statement did not sound so world-shaking as it really was to the young woman whom it concerned. For her it was cataclysmic. After she had read it again, for perhaps the tenth time, she flung herself across the bed and lay with her head buried in her arms, trying to still her nervous trembling.

It was almost too good to be believed! She had hoped that someday, some distant day, she could secure such a position, but with two older women in the department she had not dreamed of an early promotion. How she wished her mother and father were here to share her happiness! She had wanted all her life to bring to them some achievement, some honor she had earned, that she might make them as proud of her as they had often been of Jim. Now she had a trophy to lay at their feet, for it was no small honor to have been appointed head of the English department of Claremont High School with its thousands of students and its reputation for having the best English department of any school in the suburbs that clustered around the great city. Such an appointment was a special honor to one who had taught only three years.

She lay with the letter in her hand and thought of the various possibilities that might stem from this position. Increased salary, of course,—opportunity to inaugurate some of her own methods—the right to try out new ideas. As head of the department she would get a leave of absence occasionally to take a course at some university. There would be contacts with other department heads of other schools. There were unlimited possibilities. The position would broaden her entire life. Perhaps she could go to England with the group of teachers who were planning such a trip for next year. She thought about her bitter disappointment when she had been forced to relinquish her plans for a trip

to the Pacific Northwest this summer because she had to keep
house for Kit and the boys while Mother went to be with
Dad. If she had gone, she might never have had this chance,
for she remembered now that last week when she had attended a concert with Mr. Willis, the young assistant
principal of Claremont, he had questioned her rather closely
about her plans for her career, and had expressed surprise
when she had told him that she expected to teach English
all her life.

"What!" he had teased. "No matrimonial plans?"

"Not one."

"That's strange. Mr. Lansing says he hates to hire good-
looking young women because they are teaching only to
earn money for a trousseau."

"Well, I'm not that kind! I teach because I want to and
like it. Even if I got married, I'd want to keep on teaching.
It's a—a—*calling* to me!"

He had laughed at her intensity, but she remembered now
that he had gone on to question her at length about her
training and her ideas. This appointment could well be
the result of that conversation. And she might have missed
it had she gone West with the girls.

Oh, but it was going to be fun to tell Mother and Dad
about this,—to show them that Ginny as well as Jimmy
could win laurels. It had been hard at times to be nothing
but Jim Martin's sister—not pretty nor plain, neither clever
nor dull, just ordinary Virginia Martin. Being ordinary
would not have been so bad if the rest of the family had been
ordinary also, but Jim had always been a leader and the
family had grown accustomed to his successes. Kurt, though
just ready for college, was showing the same qualities that
had made Jim stand out from the crowd. As for Kit—well,
she combined all the charms of both. Jim, Kurt and Kit all
had what Dad called "the Tarleton look," and the charm of
manner and air of gracious friendliness that made Mother
admired by all of her friends. Virginia and Dad were different. As a child she had been painfully shy, and had grown

up believing herself to be a sad misfit in the family. But as maturity came, she realized her likeness to her father, and because she loved him devotedly, she had set out to develop those qualities in herself that were admirable in him. She was a true Martin—quiet, unable to show her feelings easily, strong with the strength of character that was a heritage from generations of plain, God-fearing ancestors. To the family she was just Ginny, the dependable elder daughter on whom they all leaned.

Two months ago when Dad had been injured and Mother had hurried to him, it had not occurred to any of them, nor to Virginia herself, that there was anything to do except for her to relinquish her plans for the long-anticipated trip and stay at home to manage the household, and fill Mother's place as best she could. There had been nothing else to do, and Virginia had accepted the fact calmly. But alone in her room at night, she had endured dark hours of near-rebellion, especially when cards and letters came from the vacationists. Not even Jim had known how bad she had felt, though he had tried in every way he could to make the situation easier for her. Kurt, too, had helped as much as possible, and they had all stood together like soldiers when Kit had been injured. But it had been a hard summer and her disappointment had not lessened even though she had kept it hidden.

But now it was gone entirely. What a tragedy it would have been if she had gone with the girls, if she never had that talk with Howard Willis, if this wonderful thing had not happened to her! How foolish to grieve when frustrations came. How shameful that Christians should doubt when they could walk calmly with their Lord and trust Him to give to them every good and perfect gift. Never again would she doubt!

Perhaps, too, this was the opportunity about which she had been dreaming, the chance to leave some permanent record of her life here when she herself had passed on. Could there be a better place in which to leave such a memorial than the hearts and minds of youth? To teach them to know and love the good and beautiful in the literature of all ages—to help to open their souls to the beneficent influences of fellowship with the great men and women who had left their own memorial behind them in literature which would live as long as civilization remained—that was a high purpose indeed. If she could prove herself worthy of this place, might she not expect to go on someday to a full professorship in a college or university?

Kit's voice, calling from the other room, aroused her. She put the letter in her desk and decided to say nothing to Jim until she had had the interview that Mr. Lansing had requested for Friday morning. That was only two days away. Then when her contract was all signed she would spring her grand surprise. She hurried to Kit, who was sitting propped against her pillow sobbing over her letter.

"Oh, Ginny! You were so *long* coming! Ginny, do you think Mother and Daddy will *ever* come home? She says he doesn't *know* her yet."

Virginia took the letter, brushed back the tangle of hair and bathed the hot little face with a cool cloth.

"Now, Kitty-puss, if you cry every time a letter comes, we can't let you have them any more. Of course they'll be home. Mr. Hudson is expected back tonight and he will probably have good news for us. He took another doctor down and things are going to be O. K. You just wait and see."

"Do you really think so?"

"I really do. And Dr. Sawyer is coming tonight with the reports on your X-rays and all those other tests. You must hurry and get well so that when Mother and Dad get back you will be as good as new."

Kit was comforted and Virginia left her with a puzzle to solve while she did the neglected ironing. Her heart was filled with joyful anticipation of the time when Kit would be well, Mother and Dad would be home again, and she, Virginia Martin, would be head of the English department of Claremont High School.

"There'd better be a clear track on the sands of time," she said with a giggle. "Virginia Martin is getting ready to make some lasting footprints, but you can't make permanent impressions on sand, so I'll take the sharp tool of my wits and carve my name in the marble corridors of time!"

Chapter Two

The doctor had gone. Out in the driveway his car door slammed, and the two in the living room heard the engine start. The glare from the headlights swept across the window in an arc as he backed out of the driveway into the street. Then the sound of that one car mingled with the others that were passing to and fro. It was only when they knew he was far down the street that the silence inside was broken. As usual, it was Jim who spoke first. In this closely-knit brother and sister twosome he almost always led out.

"Well, that's that. Where do we go from here?"

"That's the sixty-four-dollar question. Where *do* we go?"

The two looked at each other, not in expectation of a solution to their mutual problem, but more as if for the reassurance that always came to them from each other's presence. Then Virginia spoke again.

"They don't sound so explosive when taken separately. Just a dog and a boy and a bicycle and a fat little girl on roller skates. But combined—they have surely spelled catastrophe. Eight hundred dollars' worth so far!"

"And that's only the beginning of sorrows," said Jim soberly. "Did you ever see anything more placidly smug than Doc's face when he told us what lies ahead for Kit? It's just one more interesting bone study for him. 'Byrnes from Denver is the best man in the country for that kind of surgery. He'll come on when we decide we need him.

He is reasonable, too. Will do it for a thousand dollars,
I am sure.' Just like that!"

Virginia groaned. "Jimmie, why should a mess like this
have to happen when we are holding the bag? Who was
the fellow in mythology that had a mountain piled on him?
That's me!"

"It was Pelion—no, it was Ossa. But he wasn't a fellow.
He was another mountain. Your mythology is as rotten as
your grammar. For a teacher you sure have your weak spots."

"I don't teach mythology nor yet grammar. I teach English
literature, and there's a vast difference. Anyway, it was Atlas
I was talking about. He had the world on his shoulders,
didn't he? Well, so that's *me*—and I mean me, not I."

"Wow! You're vicious! Why don't you go out and split
an infinitive and be *real* tough?"

Virginia laughed at his nonsense, but her face sobered
again at the thought of the problem facing them. There
was no denying the size nor the seriousness of that problem,
and they must face it alone and at once.

Two months ago life had been smooth and satisfying to
these young Martins. Jim was doing well in the research
laboratories of the firm which Dad had served for thirty
years, Virginia was teaching in the local high school, and
Kurt was ready to enter college. For the last few years,
since Dad had been put in charge of the Foreign Department there had been money enough to enable them to live
prosperously and graciously in this pleasant suburb of the
great city. Before that there had been other years that had
not been so easy, but the memory of them had faded. The
present had been too all-absorbing to allow thoughts of a
time less happy. That the assured current of their lives
might become suddenly disturbed did not occur to them.

When Dad decided to go to Central America to see about
the new office there, he did not expect to be gone more than
two weeks. The headlines in the morning paper one day,
telling of a plane lost over the mountains of Mexico did not
seem significant in the lives of the Martins. But when, a

few hours later, Mr. Hudson, the president of the firm, had called to tell them that Dad had been on that plane, the headline became the most important thing in their world. There followed three days of uncertainty and fear that they would never forget. Hereafter, when the story of a lost plane came to their attention they would realize the heartbreak and anguish involved, and their sympathy would go out to others who knew the grief that was now theirs.

On the fourth morning, word came through that rescuers had found the plane on an almost inaccessible plateau. Then for two more days they had alternately hoped and despaired, until the message came that had brought a measure of relief. Dad was alive, although badly hurt. He had been taken to a small mission hospital, and there he must stay until he was able to make the arduous trip down the mountains.

Mr. Hudson prepared to leave at once, and in spite of his insistence that it was not necessary and that it would be a long and difficult trip, Mother determined to go with him. For every objection that was raised she had an answer. Who would keep the house and look after their needs? Why, Mrs. Malone, of course. Who would attend to the business affairs that were bound to come up with Dad so far away and unable to do anything? Jim could do that. He was old enough to begin to take some responsibility. Who would discipline Kit? For Kit needed more discipline than a squad of Irish Regulars. Virginia could do that!

"She has always minded you better than she does me anyway," Mother had said. "She will just have to understand that you are in control. You can manage all right, children, and I have to go. I can't stay here and let him suffer there alone."

Mr. Hudson, when he found Mother to be determined, had helped to arrange their affairs. There was money enough in the bank to pay the household expenses for some time. If they had not just bought the new car and had the garage rebuilt there would have been enough to give a feeling of confidence in any eventuality, but even so, they could manage comfortably. Dad's salary must be sent to Mother, for no one could tell what circumstances she must face. Virginia and Jim would have to share the home responsibilities, financial and otherwise. Mother's instructions were thrown at them in much the same way her clothes were tossed into her suitcases. In case of real emergency they could sell some of those bonds in the vault at the bank. Jim had power of attorney—the vault key was in the little drawer of her desk—Kurt must do just as Jim said about everything—Kit would be a good girl and mind Ginny and help Mrs. Malone, wouldn't she?—there was nothing to worry about and it would all work out all right in a few weeks. Surely she would be back soon bringing Dad with her.

It was only after they had told her good-bye and she had watched the taxi disappear down the street that Virginia realized that, of course, the trip with her friends was out of the question. That she would stay at home was a foregone conclusion that had not even merited mention.

"It's just another dream that didn't materialize. I have quite a collection of them. I save them as I used to save the tragic remains of my burst balloons."

That night her pillow was wet with tears, but the next morning she was their placid Ginny again and not even Jim realized her disappointment.

The first few days after Mother had gone passed quietly. Kurt helped Jim at the factory, Virginia was busy with summer school, and Kit surprised them all by her tractability and obedience. But before word was received that the travelers had reached their destination, disaster had struck. Kit, on an errand for Mrs. Malone, was flying along on her skates. No one saw the accident and the participants could not tell just how it happened, but when the barking dog was driven away and the boy and the bicycle were lifted off the little girl, she lay in a twisted, unconscious heap.

That was eight weeks ago. Last week Kit had been brought home and carried in Jim's arms upstairs and laid on

Mother's big bed. Kurt was with her now, amusing her with a new game he had invented, while Jim and Virginia looked at each other in the living room and remembered the doctor's verdict. It had not been the favorable one they had expected. The broken leg had apparently knitted, but there was an area of infection which had not yielded to treatment.

"Bone infection can be one of the ugliest things we have to handle. If Kit were strong she would stand a good chance of licking it. But she has been through enough in the last two months to faze anyone. She is high-strung anyway, and is mighty tired of all this inactivity and pain. She's just in the condition to stew and fret herself into real trouble. If that tibia doesn't heal we'll have to operate and do some grafting. It's about a fifty-fifty proposition. Byrnes from Denver is the man for the job, and he is in England now. Let's build her up for a few months and see if the body will throw off that infection. If not—well, then we'll have to send for Byrnes. He's not only the best for the job, but he will be reasonable."

But what the doctor considered reasonable and what Jim and Virginia could pay were two different things. The weeks in the hospital, with all the extra expense of laboratory fees and special tests, with transfusions and injections, with three nurses during those first anxious weeks, had drained their bank accounts. If Mother knew, she could send them some money, for she surely could not spend much in that tiny village. But they all agreed that Mother must not know. At any time Dad might regain consciousness, and when he did, Mother would pour out the entire story at once. Mother was a dear, but had never been known to keep a secret. And whatever happened, Dad must be protected from all worry. The only way to insure his peace of mind was to keep their mother carefree, so they had all entered into a con-spiracy of silence to protect him.

"I feel like Byron's prisoner." said Jim. "The one whose hair grew white in a single night. We have a job cut out for us, Ginny gal. We have to keep up this house, feed the hungry Martin mob—I never knew before how much money can be shoveled into human stomachs. I marvel that men can support their families at all. We have to care for an invalid child and build her up for a critical operation, and we have to be prepared to pay for that operation. Also, we are supposed to keep a boy in college."

Mrs. Malone had begun to prepare Kit for sleep, and Kurt came down the stairs in time to hear Jim's outburst.

"You just quit worrying about me," he said from the doorway. "I gather from your remarks that Doc says things aren't so hot with Kit. Well, I can take care of myself. My tuition is paid. Dad sent the check before he left. I saved two hundred dollars for a motorcycle this summer. I can use that, and I'll get a job. I can work twenty hours a week and do my studying O. K. Lots of guys do." He straightened his shoulders as if to convince them that he had reached the full stature of manhood.

Jim, from the davenport, where he sat with his head in his hands looked up to say, "Attaboy!" while Virginia cried, with a tremor in her voice, "You're all right, Kurt! Now if Jimmie and I can measure up, we'll come out on top yet."

With her customary thoroughness she began to plan. She put the amount of her salary and Jim's on one side of a paper, and over against it the items of expense that must be met—food, clothing, Mrs. Malone's wages, laundry, telephone, light, fuel, insurance, doctor bills, carfare.

"What a lot of money it takes to live!" she groaned, as she compared the two tables. "Jim, can't we ask Mr. Hudson to lend us some money, or give us an advance on Dad's salary, or something?"

Jim shook his head. "No, we mustn't borrow. Dad doesn't believe in it, and it would make him have a feeling of defeat to come back here to a load of debt. Anyway, Dad isn't getting well very fast, and we might just as well face facts. It's going to be a tough pull for the business as well as for us. He's the only person who knew about that new contract, and without that it will be all Mr. Hudson can do to take care of his own troubles."

"Well, we'll have to cash the bonds then."

"Not if we can get along without it. That's all we have in reserve for the operation. If Kit doesn't get better, and if Dr. Byrnes has to come, and if some other complications come along, we could use up those bonds so fast we'd never know where they went. We have to try every other possibility first."

He studied the figures again, turning the paper this way and that, as if hoping they would read differently in a different light. When he spoke there was a note of increased discouragement in his voice.

"These figures say it can be done if we live like Spartans and work like Turks. But figures have a way of lying to me. I can always make superfine budgets on paper, but I've never made one work yet."

"This one *has* to work," said Virginia with her customary determination. "If we can't sell any bonds, and if we can't borrow the money we need, we have to earn it and save it. If it has to be done, it *can* be done!"

"Just like that!" said Jim sarcastically.

Kurt had been listening to their discussion, but now, as if he could keep quiet no longer, he burst forth. "I'm not going to college and let you two down like this! I can't make as much as you can, but I made forty dollars a week all summer and I can keep on working. You can take my two hundred—"

"Whoa there, kid!" came Jim's steadying tones. "We aren't licked yet. You're going to college in a couple of weeks. We'll find some way out. I'll go through Dad's papers and—"

"And what? Find a gold mine or a million-dollar bill? Or maybe you'll find Allie May so we can sell the farm and all be rich!"

Kurt's voice rose high and cracked in his excitement. Jim pulled him down on the davenport beside him and said kindly, "You're a good scout, kid, and if we need you, we'll let you help. I wish we could find Allie May and get that farm sold. It would be the answer to all our problems."

Virginia looked at the sheet of figures and, with her secret knowledge that her salary would show a substantial raise which was not on the paper, said optimistically, "It *can* be done and it shall be done. If we all do our best we will come out on top. And I'm going to pray and believe that Kit will do so well that Dr. Byrnes and his thousand-dollar operation won't be needed!"

Jim said nothing for a few moments. When he did speak it was as if he did it reluctantly, yet under the compulsion of necessity.

"There's another phase of the thing that's bothering me. Can you picture Kit growing strong under Mrs. Malone's care? She couldn't handle the youngster when she was well. And now, with Kit nervous and irritable and spoiled, it just can't be done. You've got to stay home with her, Ginny. No one else can keep her happy."

Virginia gazed at him in astonishment and dismay.

"Why, I can't! We have to have my salary."

"Yes. And someone has to take care of Kit. Mrs. Malone could do a better job of substituting for you at school than of caring for Kit."

"But we can't live without my salary! We haven't figured in a single thing that isn't necessary, and it will take all we both can make."

Jim groaned wearily. "I know that. But I know also that Kit and Mrs. Malone are allergic to each other. If Kit were well, we could talk Dutch to her and she'd have to behave. But the way she is now, well, remember what happened this morning when she found a bit of shell in her egg. A fit like that with only Mrs. Malone to calm her would turn into a disaster that could send her back to the hospital in a jiffy. You'll have to stay with her, Ginny."

"I may have to, but I can't. We'll just have to find someone in place of Mrs. Malone. Or we'll have to find some way to earn an extra forty a week and hire a nurse to stay

Chapter Three

K it was asleep, Mrs. Malone had gone to her own room, and Virginia busied herself with straightening the room, putting away books and puzzles, picking up scraps of paper and clearing pencils, crayons, scissors and paste from the bedside table. Her mind was constantly busy with the problem. She was not like Jim. He would do his best to solve a difficulty, but when bedtime came he could forget it in sleep. But she would lie awake all night, pondering and thinking until a solution came to her. She did not doubt that there was a solution. There *must* be one. And as she turned on the light in her own room and saw the stack of mail on her desk—the mail that had come this morning—she caught again the scent of mown grass through the window, and the solution flashed into her mind. It came with such suddenness and was so unwelcome in its bitter implications that she stood in the doorway as if stunned. Then, being Virginia, she faced it and girded herself for battle.

She was shaking with a nervous chill as she started across the room toward the bed. Why should she go to bed? She would not go to sleep. She could never sleep when she was disturbed or worried. The room was almost unbearably hot anyway, and sleep would have been difficult under any circumstance. She stood for a moment dispiritedly, then turned off the light and went quietly down the hall to the door that led out onto the flat roof over the back porch.

When the house had been remodeled last year a railing

had been put around the deck and a weatherproof floor laid. It had at once become the favorite gathering place for the family during the seasons when it was possible to use it. As Virginia came out now she became acutely lonesome for her parents. Here was Mother's deck chair and Dad's old cot where he used to love to stretch out and look at the stars. Would he ever do it again?

Recent letters from Mother had been discouraging. Dad did not know her at all. He still lay in that half coma that was indescribably pitiful and unlike him. Dad had always been so active that Virginia could not picture him as Mother was seeing him now—weak, helpless, not even recognizing the touch of Mother's hands. It must be terribly hard for Mother.

Virginia went to her mother's chair and seated herself, leaning her head back so that she faced the starry dome which stretched above her. These same stars had looked down on the earth through all the centuries that had passed since creation. They had hung there as they hung now far removed from the sorrows and strife of the little world below them. What mattered to them the frustrations and heartaches of the mortals struggling along about their petty affairs? They would pass and another generation would take their place and laugh and weep and work and worry for a few days, and then they, too, would "be gathered to their tombs by those who in their turn should follow them." Man was, after all, an exceedingly small part of God's universe. Could it matter much what became of him? Was it his part to live for a season here and then pass on, leaving behind him no mark to show that he had passed that way, forgotten in a few years even by those who had walked with him? Somewhere, behind those stars, beyond the vastness of the starlit heaven, God dwelt. Tonight He seemed very far away—too far to care for Virginia or her problems.

Those problems were real and pressing. Virginia had the answer, but it was an answer that she did not want to acknowledge. Kurt's remark about Allie May must have suggested it to her, and the smell of the dead, dew-wet grass had brought it to consciousness. Until Allie May, the cousin who had been lost to them for many years, could be found, the farm must not be sold, at least not until twenty years had passed. Just now the house was empty, as the farm land had been rented to a neighbor who had his own home, and in that quiet country region there was no demand for an old, isolated, run-down farmhouse. Virginia could take Kit to the farm and live there during those weeks when she must have special care. The housing shortage here was so acute that a large furnished house like this one could be rented for a price sufficient to keep her and Kit in that out-of-the way place. Jim could get a room somewhere or even live in the little room at the labratory which he sometimes occupied when he had been working late or the weather was bad. This would take care of all of them. Mrs. Malone would be glad to be relieved of her position, and her wages could be taken off the expense side of their budget. It was as simple as that—the solution to their problem—and Virginia knew that was the way it must be. But her heart was bitter and sick within her, for on her would fall the cost that must be paid. She must write to her principal and tell him that she would not be available for teaching this fall. Someone else would be given the post that was rightly hers, and later she would return to the drudgery of teaching grammar to unenthusiastic freshmen. Such an opportunity as she was rejecting would never come again. She knew that. The years would go on and on, one after another, and she would be caught in them like a squirrel on a wheel.

Another realization came to her with a sharp thrust of pain. Her friendship with Howard Willis was becoming most interesting. They had much in common, and during the past year they had shared several enjoyable evenings together at concerts, lectures, or riding into the country. She knew that the other teachers were beginning to link their names, and she, herself, had detected a new warmth in Howard's attentions this summer. But she well knew that if she left the city for several months, Howard Willis would not be interested in a "correspondence courtship." There would be too many young women about him who would be willing to help him find entertainment in his spare time. She could name several at Claremont who would be glad to be drafted for such service.

Oh, why did *she* always have to be the one to make sacrifices and change her plans? As she looked back over her life it seemed to be a great chain of frustrations. Every time she made some plan, or built some air castle, or indulged in some dear dream, she had to give it up or adapt it to a smaller, duller pattern. Her plans and hopes were like the houses she had tried to build with a set of blocks when she was a tiny girl. She could see herself, in memory, as she labored over those houses, hoping each time that this one would become, under her fat little hands, a castle like the picture on the lid of the box in which the blocks had come. But every time she built the house to a promising height and was beginning to believe that she could finish it, it would tumble or Jim would come by and send it crashing with a slight touch of his hand. He would laugh and say with the superiority of six years over four, "Now make it over again. You didn't start right." She could remember even now the helpless hurt of that little girl as she gathered up her blocks to start another castle. That long-ago hurt returned to her and grew into utter heart-sickness as she realized that the early scene had set a pattern for her life.

There was the time when she was eight, and she and Jim had spent the summer on the farm. Allie May lived on that farm with Great Grandfather Martin, and the three children had enjoyed a never-to-be-forgotten time. When they left to return to the city, Aunt Alice had promised that Allie May should spend two weeks with them at Christmastime. That had seemed the most incredibly delightful thing that could possibly happen. Virginia had gone to sleep night after night planning the good times they would have. She had cleaned the playroom and kept it in that condition all fall.

She had saved her allowance that Allie May might help her to spend it. She had boasted, until her friends all became tired of hearing her, of the wonderful cousin who was coming. She had begun to count the days and had them down to fifty-seven when the telephone call came which had sent that dream tumbling. Uncle Fred was dead. Then had come word that Allie May and Aunt Alice didn't live with Grandpa any more, and Allie May didn't answer the letter she laboriously wrote to her. Then Grandpa had died also, and when Daddy came from the funeral he had said that Aunt Alice and Allie May were gone. There would be no more happy summers on the farm.

Another memory that came back to taunt her tonight as she sat in the deck chair on the roof under the August stars was that of her last year in high school. She had longed desperately to distinguish for herself. Jim had won many honors in his school work, and had graduated from high school as valedictorian of his class. She did not hope to achieve that. Her grades were good, but for four years the entire class had known that Clara Reece would win the coveted first place. Virginia had said to herself as a freshman, "It *would* be my luck to be in the class with a brain like Clara!" But there was one thing she could do: she could play the piano better than anyone else in the class. If she could sit at the grand piano and play while the faculty and class members marched into the assembly hall, she would achieve real distinction. She would *much* rather do that than speak! For four years she worked toward that goal. But she never achieved it. A new principal decreed that all the class members must be in the procession, and a junior was chosen to play. Virginia became just one of the three hundred students who sat through a long and wearying program and marched like wooden men to receive diplomas. "Virginia Martin also graduated," she muttered.

Another dream during her high-school days was that of going to Clearwater College with Sara Cunningham as roommate. Mother had gone to Clearwater for two happy years, and Virginia had heard again and again of the joys of life at Clearwater, until there had developed around the very name an aura of splendor. She and Sara had planned it in detail—their wardrobes, their room furnishings, their courses of study. Even the disappointment over the commencement exercises had faded into the background as preparations for college went on apace. That was the summer Kit was ill, and Dad's firm had that awful explosion and fire. When it came time to enroll there was no money for Clearwater, and Virginia had to go to City College, while Betty Harriman took her place as Sara's roommate.

She had never been able to talk to others of her disappointments. Perhaps if she had not cared so deeply it would have been easier to speak of them. But when things meant a great deal to her she could not discuss them. She seemed to freeze up inside, and a great cold lump would come where her heart should have been. If Jim were frustrated or disappointed he would do something about it—either fight for what he considered his rights or find some other plan and put it over with zest. But Virginia could only hide her hurt, pick up her blocks and try again.

This time she felt that she lacked the will to go on, for the dream that she must relinquish was, she was sure, the dearest and brightest one she had ever had. Even the thought of achieving such a position at some future, far-distant date had been a star to guide and inspire her on many a dull and weary day. Now to have come so close as almost to grasp it and then to have it fade like a mirage was worse than not to have dreamed at all. When, for the first time in her life, she was becoming interested in a man who seemed to return that interest, it made the blow doubly hard. She had always had boy friends and had enjoyed them as she did Jim, but she had never "gone steady" with any boy, even in her college days. Since she had been teaching she had been too busy and satisfied with her work to think of any special friendships with the young men she met at church or an occasional social affair. But Howard Willis' attentions had wakened her to new desires and an appreciation of his comradeship. She realized, as she sat alone in the dark, how dearly she had prized that friendship. If she went to the farm even for a few weeks—and it would probably be months rather than weeks—it would certainly be damaging to all the plans she had built around her life as a teacher. In other words—it would be just another block house!

Then—she never knew why—into her mind came the thought of the sermon she had heard the night before. The preacher had spoken of a trip he had made through the stockyards. He had seen lambs being led to slaughter and noted their meek submissiveness. Then he had told of being on a farm the year before when some young cattle were to be killed, and he had seen their struggle.

"How like those cattle we are!" he said. "The Lamb of God went to the altar of sacrifice for us. He died that we might live. He did it voluntarily, meekly submissive to the will of God that He must die to save a lost world. He did not fight against the sacrifice nor draw back from the Cross. He bore the suffering to the last agonizing pain. And He did it as the Lamb of God, in quiescent obedience to His Father. But we Christians—"dumb, driven cattle," as one poet calls us—go to our smaller sacrifices pulling back, reluctant, rebellious and sometimes defiant. We are not willing to give ourselves for service to Him who gave Himself for our salvation. He poured out His life completely for us. We shrink from one small sacrifice for Him. The life of a Christian should be one glad and continual sacrifice for the Beloved."

He had pleaded with his young people to surrender their lives and wills to the Master's call, to stand ready for any service that He might require of them, to go or stay at His command, to stand valiantly in the battle, whether at the front or in the unappreciated tasks at the rear. Jim and Kurt and Virginia had stood with many others to pledge themselves to such obedience, and Virginia had gone home wondering what the first call would be. Well, here it was, and she did not want to submit at all. She wanted to pull back and rebel, like the frightened cattle, against her lot. *Why* did it have to be *this*? And why did she, instead of Jim or Kurt, have to be the one to give up her plans? It seemed it had always been so. Jim hadn't cared to go away to college. City College had satisfied him. Jim had just *walked* away with scholastic honors all his life. And now Jim would get to stay on his job, and would be near Dot Blackwell, around whom his life seemed to revolve these days, while she, Virginia would have to go away from everything she loved and *stagnate* in a farmhouse that had neither plumbing nor electricity and was heated by a coal stove in the middle of the living room. Oh, how she hated it all! It had to be done, and she would do it. But she wouldn't like it. She wouldn't even *try* to like it!

A noise from the room where Kit lay startled her. She hurried inside feeling guilty as she saw the clock on the dresser. She had been on the roof almost two hours! The bedroom was hot after the pleasant coolness outside, and Kit's tumbled pillows showed that she had been restless. As Virginia stooped over to smooth the pillow she noticed that the little girl's cheeks were unnaturally red and the eyelids swollen.

"Kit, have you been crying? What is it, dear? Does your leg hurt?"

"It always hurts," came a shaky voice. "But I don't cry over it. I'm not a baby! The nurses at the hospital say I'm *brave*."

"You are. You're a little soldier. But why are you crying, honey? Can't you tell Ginny?"

"I've just been thinking,—and—oh, thinking's so *sad*."

"Why, you poor chickie! What sad thoughts are troubling you? Come on. Tell your pal."

Virginia smoothed back the tangled curls and Kit drew a quick breath.

"It's so awful, the things I think about. About Mother being away—and Daddy never knowing us again—and about—a—a—

little girl who had to have her leg cut off!" Her voice broke completely and she clung to Virginia in a paroxysm of sobs. Virginia gathered her close and said soothingly, "You poor lamb! I should have been in here with you. Now we're going to change those thoughts. In the first place, whatever made you think about a leg that was cut off? That's nonsense!"

"Well, the doctor said he might operate. When they operated on Kurt they cut out his appendix!"

"That's entirely different. His appendix was no good at all. But your leg is. If the doctor operates, he will just put in a new piece of bone in place of a bad bit. But we don't think he will have to operate at all. He says that if you will just get well and strong your leg will heal by itself. So you and I are going out to Grandpa's farm and live there a while. It's a fine place for little girls. I'm sure that if we live there, and you try real hard to grow strong, the doctor won't have to do anything."

"Really, Ginny? The farm where you and Jim used to play with Allie May?"

"The very same. And you are going to get so well there that when Mother and Daddy come home they won't be able to tell that you've been ill. It's hard now, honey, but after a while everything is going to be—"

"Hunky-dory!" cried Kit, her sorrows forgotten.

"Yes, that's it. Go to sleep and tomorrow I'll tell you a story about how we once played Robinson Crusoe on the pond at the farm."

Kit closed her eyes and Virginia sat watching until she fell asleep. What a dear she was! What mattered a few months of her own life compared with the health and well-being of this beloved baby sister? This task was hers. She would do it well and would go obediently to the altar. But she didn't have to *like* it!

Chapter Four

It was a warm, hazy day in early October when the car drove down the unpaved street at the edge of the little town where Grandpa Martin's old house stood. The ninety-mile trip had been almost like a picnic, for both Virginia and Jim had endeavored to hide from Kit their depression at the change in their lives. Since the decision had been made, Kit's spirits and, as a consequence, her health, had improved greatly. The thought of going to the farm about which she had heard so many fascinating stories was a stimulus that did more for her than the doctor's prescriptions. She did not realize that it could be anything but a pleasure to all, and they did not disillusion her. As they drove along they had joked and chattered, played games with the letters on the signboards along the way, gathered red leaves and bittersweet berries from the woods, and stopped at a wayside stand to buy apples, nuts and cider.

"If we're going to farm we want to have a well-stocked cellar," Virginia said.

Now, just at noon, they turned from the street into the long lane that led to the house. The car jolted and bumped over the ruts and Kit, propped among the pillows on the back seat, winced in pain.

"They don't have—good pavements—here." She gasped.

"No, to put it mildly, they don't. This road was first made by the wheels of a covered wagon probably. And even when Granddad got his old Ford he never changed it. Can't you remember him, Ginny, sitting like a ramrod on the seat of that high old car? He'd set his mouth in a straight line and glue his eyes to the road, and no one in the car dared say a word while he was driving!"

"Oh, don't I remember!" said Virginia, with a laugh. "Once I wouldn't be still and he stopped the car and spanked me!"

Kit forgot her pain at the thought of anyone's spanking Virginia.

"I wish I had been big enough to know Grandpa," she said. "I was born too late for all the fun."

The car drew up at the steps of the long porch which extended across one entire side of the house.

Jim looked at his watch as he stepped from the car. "We're a bit early. The lawyer was to meet us here at twelve-thirty with the key. Times have changed even here if they need keys. Granddad never had one."

"It's grand in this sunshine," said Virginia, looking around as if eager to go exploring among these scenes which seemed like a dream out of a dim past. But at that moment the door of the house opened, and a man came out, saying, with an embarrassed smile, "I didn't mean to be caught in your house. I was just giving it a last-minute check-up to see that it was O. K. I'm Barrett, your lawyer."

Virginia shook hands with him gravely, stifling an impulse to laugh. She had expected to see a tall, stoop-shouldered man in a faded black suit, carrying his papers in a brief case that seemed always bursting at the seams. It had not occurred to her that Grandpa's lawyer might have been replaced, during these years by another. Nor did Mr. Barrett resemble her picture of a lawyer.

"I opened the house to air a bit; then I built a fire in the dining room. It's warm out in the sunshine, but the house seemed too cool for the little girl," he said, with a smile for Kit.

"Thank you for your thoughtfulness," said Virginia. "I'm sure we shall need it as the sun gets lower."

Jim had opened the car door and reached for Kit's crutches, but Mr. Barrett was at his side, and before Kit realized what was happening she had been lifted in his arms and carried across the porch into the dining room where she was deposited in a big armchair that Jim drew up to the fire.

"Oh, I like a fire up in the house where you can see it!" she exclaimed. "But you don't have to carry me, Mr. Barrett. I can walk on my crutches."

"Sure you can." agreed Jim. "But just for this once you got carried,—just like a bride entering her new home."

Kit giggled and Mr. Barrett blushed. Virginia, to relieve him, said hastily "You rest a while in front of this fire, Kitkin, and then you can mount those crutches and explore all these downstairs rooms."

"Oh, goody, I want to see them all. Is this house ours? I like it. Why didn't I ever see it before?"

"Well, Grandpa Martin, who owned it, died years before you were born. Dad has had a strange family living in it, so we didn't visit them."

"Where is that family?"

"They bought a farm of their own," said Mr. Barrett, coming in the door with a big box from the car. "This year it was rented to a neighbor who had his own house."

"I'm glad he didn't want it. I *like* it here."

"So you've said several times." Jim deposited the last of the suitcases on the floor. "Have you got plenty of bedding, Ginny?"

"There are many blankets in the closet in the back hall." explained the young lawyer, "and also several closets full upstairs. I got Aunt Molly Haley to come over on Monday and Tuesday, and she cleaned and aired the whole house. Things are just as they were here when the old man died. The couple that had the place until this year lived in these two rooms and the rest of the house has been shut up. I think you'll find everything that you need. We didn't dare sell anything until we could find the other heir."

"Any trace of her?" asked Virginia, struggling with the knots that tied a huge box.

"Here, let me do that. No clue as yet. I've been going over the papers since I took over after my father's death, and I can find nothing encouraging. Your father wrote me last spring, urging me to the utmost effort, but I've made no progress. Seventeen years is a long time. A person can travel quite a distance in that time, and your cousin Allie May seems to have spent most of those years going away from here at a high rate of speed. But we're still looking and I hope to find her yet."

"And in the meantime it's lucky for us that she wasn't found as we need this house for the next few months."

Jim returned from an exploratory trip to the kitchen and pantry. "The old cooky jar is still there but it's as empty as my stomach. Can't I go to town and buy your supplies, Ginny? I have to start back to the city before long. There's all my junk to be moved over to the laboratory yet. I promised to turn over the house keys at nine tomorrow morning. Will you get a list ready? Or can't I stay with Kit while you shop? Can you negotiate those ruts?"

"Of course I can."

"Why should you?" asked Mr. Barrett. "I would be glad to drive you into town. I know where the stores are and I can introduce you to the proprietors."

"Do I have to be introduced? I never had to at the stores in the city."

"You don't have to here, but many of the people in our little town were friends of your grandfather and will be glad to know you and to serve you."

While Jim unpacked the boxes with Kit watching from her chair, Virginia and Mr. Barrett shopped.

"Hereafter when you have to go into town, telephone me and I'll have Aunt Molly go over and sit with your little sister. The grocer will deliver your orders so you won't have to carry them."

"Do we have a telephone?"

"There's an old-fashioned instrument behind the kitchen door. I'll have it connected at once. I'll tell them it's an emergency. You mustn't be there alone with a sick child and no telephone."

"You're certainly very thoughtful of us."

"Your Great-grandfather Martin was my grandfather's client for over fifty years. They died the same year. My father handled the estate for your father for fifteen years, and after he was gone I fell heir to it. We've always thought of the Martins as more than clients. They were friends. I'd like to do anything I can to help out. I hope you'll call on me if you need anything."

"I probably will. I'm a greenhorn about country life. I just happened to think that I don't know how to build a fire. And I never lit a kerosene lamp in my life."

"You'll do all right. I'll lay the kitchen fire when we get back and you'll be able to do it the next time."

When Virginia saw him do it she was not so sure that she could be successful "the next time." But she said nothing and determined that she would practice until she was an expert fire-builder. While she prepared the lunch Jim and Mr. Barrett stored the supplies in the pantry, Jim taking delight in opening several boxes of cookies and putting them in the old blue jar.

"These things are a poor substitute for the ones Aunt Alice used to keep in here. Next time I come I want to find some ginger ones sprinkled with sugar."

Mr. Barrett staved for lunch, as Jim had some business pertaining to the estate to discuss with him. They had a jolly meal by the sunny dining-room window. It was all a thrilling adventure to Kit. After they had eaten she consented to Virginia's suggestion that she rest on the couch, and before the business discussion was ended she was fast asleep.

Virginia dared not let Jim know how lonely she felt as she watched him prepare to leave. Mr. Barrett had gone, the luggage was all inside, the shopping done, and there was no further reason for Jim to delay.

"You don't mind, do you?" he asked anxiously. "You won't be frightened here alone?"

"Of course not! What could harm us?"

"Nothing, really. But everything is so different from home, and the place is sort of isolated. I'm glad Barrett's getting the phone fixed. He said to tell you that Grandpa's old ring was one long and two short. The phone was disconnected only last spring when the tenants left, so it's listed with that ring. Can't you remember how we used to listen for that 'one long and two short'?"

"No, I can't remember the phone at all, but I'll be listening for that ring. Call me up occasionally, Jimmy. There will be no one else to use the phone."

"Will do. I think Steve Barrett will probably keep in close touch with you, too. He takes his responsibilities as our lawyer very seriously, and between looking after you, hunting for Allie May and worrying over Dad, he will be kept busy. I hope he has some other clients, though. I don't want his full support to come out of our pockets."

Virginia laughed. "He did spend a lot of time on us today, didn't he? I can't think of him as a lawyer. He looks more like a farmer. A lawyer in khaki slacks and a tee shirt is a bit irregular, isn't he?"

"Seems so. But he's a regular guy, at that. No Adonis like your intellectual friend, and no personality boy, but the kind of chap you could call on for anything you need and he'd be Johnny-on-the-spot."

"O.K. I'll forgive your slam at my friend and will promise to call on Steve Barrett when in distress. His looks and personality won't make any difference if the chimney smokes or the roof leaks."

"Well, I'll have to be going." Jim's face sobered and he put his arm around her. "This whole business is tough, and it's Ginny who bears the load, as usual. I wish I could do it."

"You know you couldn't, so let's not think about it. You will have plenty of problems yourself, Jimmy. Kurt is your

job, as Kit is mine. With keeping an eye on him, taking
care of taxes and upkeep on the house and managing all
Dad's other affairs, you won't have any snap."

"You're a brick! When this is all over you and I are
going to celebrate."

"You aren't half bad yourself. Now run along, and don't
worry about us. We'll be fine."

He kissed her soberly, gave her a reassuring pat on the
arm, and ran for his car. She watched his tortuous progress
down the rutted lane, waved to him as he turned into the
street, and gazed until he disappeared from sight. Then
she turned back to the room where Kit—precious, lovable,
difficult Kit—lay asleep in trustful security. Ginny was in
charge of things and Kit could sleep with no thought of
ill. If only she, Virginia, could find that sweet assurance! If
only she could feel as sure of God as Kit felt of her Ginny!
But God seemed to her not one on whom she could lean in
trust and safety but a strange Being who let her fall with
a sharp jolt when she leaned on Him.

"Maybe when I'm ninety years old and am dying in an
old ladies' home I'll understand *why* life is like this. But just
now all I know is that I don't like it!"

Then, being Ginny, she set about taking charge of the
situation. She longed to investigate the other rooms of the
house, for she had been so young when she had spent her
summers here that even the arrangement of the rooms was
a hazy memory. She wanted to wander through them and
see what forgotten scenes and happenings would return to
her. But she must not do that now for fear that Kit would
waken while she was away and be frightened by the solitude,
so she busied herself by carrying the suitcases into the downstairs bedroom, which they would have to use because Kit
was unable to climb stairs.

As she entered the large room with its high walnut bed
and old-fashioned wardrobe, she felt a reassuring sense
of familiarity. She remembered it now! This was Grandpa's
room. Jim used to share it with him. That last summer

Grandpa had usually gone to bed early, before Aunt Alice had been able to corral the three wild youngsters. He did not go to sleep early, but merely lay down to rest, he said. After the children had been called from their play and made to wash their hands and feet at the bench by the cistern, they would tiptoe in and sit on the bed and tell Grandpa the day's happenings. Then Jim would bring the Bible and light the lamp on the bureau and Grandpa would read to them just as he used to read when Dad and Uncle Fred were little boys. When he had finished they would kneel by his bed while he prayed.

Virginia's heart was stirred by this memory. What a grand old Grandpa he had been! No wonder Dad, was a stalwart Christian, having been reared by such a grandfather. She wished now that she could remember more of the days she had spent with him. Perhaps when Jim came back he could help her to recall many things that she had lost in the shadows of the past.

Virginia hurried about, hanging dresses in the closet and piling clothes in the deep drawers of the bureau. The silence in the house was oppressive and she wished Kit would waken. How comforting it would be to hear automobile horns honking on the boulevard or the clang of a street-car gong around the corner. But the street was only a dirt road and the town did not boast a carline. If only some sound —any sound—would break this deadly stillness. She decided to go back to the dining room and unpack books. The work in the bedroom could wait until Kit was awake and could watch her.

She must get out some blankets first, however, so that they could air. Mr. Barrett had said they were in the closet. Where *was* the closet where Aunt Alice used to keep bedding? Oh, yes, at the end of the hall! She must hurry for she heard Kit stirring. The hall was dim for the afternoon had waned and twilight was near. She had forgotten that there was a mirror in the closet door, and she stopped now in sudden shock as she found herself gazing into the startled

Chapter Five

Late that night, long after Kit was asleep at her side, Virginia lay wide awake. She wished she had left a light burning, for the silence and darkness pressed about her until she could almost feel the weight of them. But she could not sleep well while a kerosene lamp burned. She had her flashlight but did not want to weaken its bulb by overuse, so she lay tense in the darkness and wished for a sound in the stillness. When she did hear a noise, she sat up in bed with rapidly beating heart, for the creaking of boards sounded to her like the tread of cautious feet in the room overhead. Several times she heard it; then silence closed in again. She lay down, scolding herself for her timidity. Of course it was only the wind which had risen as evening drew on and was now tossing the branches of the trees outside the window. What would the boys think if they knew what a "fraidy cat" she had become? At last she drifted into sleep that was broken and uncomfortable.

In the heavy dark that comes with the early hours before dawn Virginia struggled into wakefulness, wondering where she was and what had roused her. She reached for the switch of the table lamp by her bed but her hand touched the end of the bureau. Then she sat up quickly as she realized that Kit, by her side, was sobbing into her pillow.

"What is it, honey?" she asked anxiously.

"Are you awake? I'm glad, but I wasn't going to call you. My leg hurts so *much*. It just hurts and hurts!"

41

"I'm sorry, darling. Will it help if I rub it? Or shall I get the heating pad," Then she remembered that the pad would be useless in a house with no electricity. She massaged the aching leg and placed a large pillow under it to support it. But the pain continued and Kit became almost hysterical.

"I can't stand it! I can't! And I want my mother and daddy," she wailed.

"Kittykin, I'm sorry as can be. But you know that Mother and Daddy can't come. I think that long ride yesterday was too much for this poor leg. I'm going out to the kitchen and heat some water and fix up the hot-water bottle for you."

She left the lamp on the dresser and, by the aid of the flashlight, made her way to the kitchen, remembering that she and Jim had investigated the operation of the small kerosene stove which stood in the pantry. The water in the reservoir at the back of the old range might still be a bit warm from the fire that had been in the stove at suppertime. If so, she should be able to get hot water in a few minutes. Oh, for a gas or electric range, or, better yet, a faucet that would produce steaming water.

In the faint glow cast by the flashlight the kitchen seemed eerie and forlorn, and she hastened to light the lamp in the wall bracket over the table. But as she touched the chimney her hand drew back in quick reaction. Then she stiffened in panic. The lamp chimney was hot! Not just warm as if the lamp had been lighted some time ago, but *hot,* as if it had just been blown out. She stood as if frozen in her tracks. From the dining room she could hear the slow *tick-tock, tick-tock* of the old clock on the mantel, and beyond that, in the bedroom, Kit's moaning sobs. Everywhere else in the old house was silence. Yet there was someone here—someone who did not belong here and yet had been in this kitchen in the last few minutes.

It seemed to Virginia that she could not move, either to heat the water or to return through that dark dining room and down the long hall to—She drew in her breath sharply and clenched her hands in the effort it took to refrain from screaming, for a sudden picture had come to her mind of that hall mirror and the girl she had seen there. In the half-light she had thought it was her own reflection. But now, in her fright she recalled the image clearly—a dark-haired girl with a white collar. And yesterday she had worn her blue crepe *without* its customary collar! She was shaking with fright and her impulse was to run, to run out of this house, anywhere, to get away from this unknown being who hid in closets, walked about at midnight and haunted the kitchen at four o'clock in the morning. But Kit was suffering and must be helped.

With shaking, clammy hands Virginia lit the lamp. The doors were all closed, the shades drawn, and there seemed nothing amiss in the kitchen. When the water was hot she decided to leave the lamp burning. If she had to make another trip out here tonight it would be much easier to come back to a lighted room.

When the hot-water bottle had been tucked against the aching limb, Kit drew a quavering breath of relief. Virginia held her close and sang softly the old song that had been a favorite in Kit's babyhood.

> Sleep, baby, sleep! Thy father guards his sheep;
> Thy mother is shaking the dreamland tree,
> And down falls a pretty dream for thee:
> Sleep, baby, sleep.

Gradually the sobs ceased, the tense nerves relaxed, and Kit was asleep. Virginia lay quietly, fearful lest she rouse the child again. When she had come from the kitchen she had drawn the heavy bolt on the bedroom door, and the windows were fastened with a catch that allowed an opening of only an inch or two. Surely no one could enter this room. She thought of how trustfully Kit slept, and wished she might be a child again with no responsibilities to rest like lead on her heart. She recalled with homesick longing the home they had left a few hours ago, with its shady green lawn, its broad terrace, the living room with its deep comfortable chairs, its soft rugs and lovely curtains, the shelves of books, the grand piano by the west window where the best light fell. She thought of the sun deck over the porch, where they would all gather on summer evenings, and like an overpowering breaker, a wave of yearning for her parents came over her. Kit was not the only one who wanted Mother and Dad!

She dared not cry lest she waken Kit, so she turned her face into her pillow and prayed.

"Dear God take care of us all. We're so far apart and in trouble and we need Thee *so* much. Please make Kit and Dad well and bring us together again. And help me to be brave and able to do the things I have to do. Amen."

She knew it wasn't a well-phrased prayer. It sounded more like that of a primary child than an English teacher in a large school. But it banished somewhat the loneliness of that dark hour, and brought a sense of peace that enabled her to go to sleep.

Chapter Six

"Ginny, oh, Ginny, wake up! It's been morning for hours and I want to get up."

Virginia tore herself reluctantly from the hold of sleep and turned over to look at the clock on the bureau.

"It can't be!" she gasped. "That clock says nine o'clock. It must be wrong."

"No, it isn't. Your watch says the same and the clock in the dining room just struck. I've been listening to it for *hours!* It sounds awful—like the one in the book of poetry, saying, 'Forever, never, never, forever.' Don't you remember, Ginny? It's in the red Longfellow book in Dad's set of poets. It makes me think it's talking about him and Mother and saying they'll never get home."

"None of that foolish talk, Kitty. You promised. I'm sorry to be so late. Why didn't you wake me sooner? You're probably hungry."

"Hungry? Why, I'm like Kurt would say 'in the last stages of starvation.' But I didn't call you because I was ashamed for keeping you awake in the night."

"Why, thats all right, pussy! I didn't mind that."

"Well, you sure looked all done in when you brought the hot-water bottle. And that's what made me ashamed, 'cause the leg didn't hurt *quite* as much as you thought it did. It hurt lots, but my inside hurt most."

"Your inside? Were you sick?"

"Not really sick; just misrable. I won't tell what I thought

45

about most, 'cause you reminded me that I promised. But I didn't promise not to talk about how different this place is from home. I liked it yesterday, and I think I'm going to like it today. But last night it felt spooky. And it sounded spooky, and it even *smelt* spooky!"

"Sounds like a slight touch of homesickness instead of an infected leg, and I'm relieved. I guess I *was* pretty sleepy when you called me but I don't want you ever to keep still if you feel 'misrable' in the night."

Virginia unlocked the door, threw wide the window to let in the clean October air, and then they started for the kitchen, Kit's crutch making a rythmic thump as she hurried down the hall.

"Don't I sound like a pegleg!" she giggled. "Pegleg Martin, that's me! Er—I mean 'I'!"

The sun was shining, and through the frame of the dining-room window the maple tree by the door made a crimson and gold picture. With the brightness outside and the gay little girl inside, the atmosphere was so cheerful that Virginia began to wonder if the fear during the dark hours of the night was all a dream. But when she reached the kitchen her confidence received a shock, for in the old iron sink stood a cereal bowl with a spoon in it—a bowl that had not been washed. Virginia knew that she had not left such a bowl in that place. The sink had been left clean and empty last night when she finished the dishes. She went about the preparations for breakfast, not letting Kit see her concern. During the meal she joined in the child's merriment, and laughed and talked as if this were a pleasure jaunt rather than the sternly necessary undertaking it was.

But in the back of her mind was always the consciousness of that hot lamp chimney and the unwashed cereal dish. Furthermore, the bottle of milk that she had opened for Kit's bedtime glass had less in it than it should. Try as she would to keep her thoughts occupied, she caught herself listening for steps overhead, and as soon as she could do so without attracting Kit's attention she bolted the stair door. She wondered why Grandpa's father, when he built this house more than a hundred years ago, had put bolts on every door, inside and out. But whatever his reason she was glad of it now.

When the telephone bell rang, both she and Kit were startled, for its shrill jangle was startlingly different from the telephones to which they were accustomed. For the moment she had forgotten that the telephone was to be connected today. But Steve Barrett's voice reassured her. He was inquiring about how they were and if they would like to have Aunt Molly Haley deliver milk and eggs as they needed them. It was a commonplace inquiry, from a common-place country lawyer, but this morning he was a most welcome contact with a world that seemed too far from them.

"I promised your brother that I would help you whenever possible," he said, as if in apology for this early call. "But I won't know what you need unless you tell me. I hope you will feel free to do that at any time."

Virginia wondered what he would think if she told him that she was afraid to stay there, that the house was haunted. But she thanked him for his kindness and promised him she would call upon him whenever she needed help. As she turned from the phone, Kit said, "That was Mr. Barrett, wasn't it? He's not a very glamrus person, but it's nice to have somebody call, anyway, isn't it?"

"Yes, indeed. I'm glad for that old phone. And it's certainly kind of Mr. Barrett to be so thoughtful of us."

All morning as she went about her unfamiliar tasks in this unfamiliar atmosphere she puzzled over the events of the past night or looked forward with dread to the coming one. How could she go to bed and to sleep knowing that there might be—there surely was—someone else in the house where she and Kit were supposed to be alone? She thought she knew how pioneer women felt when they had to barricade themselves and fight off Indians. A visible Indian might not be so fearsome as this unknown being.

After noon, when the sun had warmed the air, she took

Kit out on the porch. The house sheltered them from the wind and, snug in their jackets and scarfs, they did not mind the slight chill. It was the first time Kit had had the opportunity to view the surrounding landscape, and she gazed on it with lively interest. Virginia saw several landmarks that were familiar to her and pointed them out to Kit.

"That white house on the hill beyond the creek is where Allie May's other grandpa used to live. Jim and I envied her because she had two grandpas and we only one. And the bridge over the creek was our ship. We sailed all over the world on it."

"Like a fellow I read about on a merry-go-round. You paid your money and took your ride 'and where's you been?'" Kit laughed.

"Exactly, but it was lots of fun. The cupola on the barn here by the orchard was one of our favorite spots. It was our lookout when we played games."

"What games?"

"Pirate and Indian and Civil War and lots of things. Once we were Perry's crew finding the North Pole."

"Who's 'we'?"

"You know. Jim and I and Allie May?"

"Oh, why was I born so late? All the fun was used up when I got here. Even Kurt used to visit here when he was a baby."

Virginia laughed at Kit's gloom and said soothingly, "You and I are going to have some fine times here. And probably it won't be long until you will be climbing into that cupola yourself."

"Do you honestly think so, Ginny?"

"I surely do. We are going to work hard at this business of helping the leg get well, and when Mom and Dad come home you'll be as good as new!"

Kit, cheered by this optimism, hobbled the length of the porch several times for exercise. Virginia let her eyes rove over the view that she had not beheld for many years. There was little change. Behind them lay the small town with its shady dooryards and wide streets. Before them the fields stretched down to the creek, then up the hill to the fence that marked the limits of Grandpa's farm. Beyond that the road led to the white house on the hill. She wondered if Allie May's grandfather still lived there. Of couse not; else the lawyers could have found Allie May. When Aunt Alice took Allie May away Grandpa and Grandma Ormand must have gone, too.

Behind the Ormand house the gold and red and brown of the wooded hills made a gorgeous backdrop, above which the October sky stretched like a blue canopy. The air was crisp and clean, and Virginia drew deep breaths, filling her lungs with the tangy freshness. The entire scene was so peaceful that she felt ashamed of the fear that had been hers last night. Whoever the intruder may have been, she was surely gone, and would not return.

"Ginny, look! See the little weeny house down against the hill? See it? The little brown one. Isn't it cute? I wonder who lives there."

"I see it. Yes, it looks almost like a doll house, snuggling at the foot of that hill. I think that must be where Mrs. Haley lives, the one who cleaned and aired our house for Mr. Barrett. I think she was one of Grandma's friends."

"Oh, do you remember Grandma, too?"

"Just a little bit. She was always in bed. She died when I was five. A little lady used to visit Aunt Alice and talk about Grandma. That must have been Mr. Barrett's Aunt Molly. Do you see the big tree that is close to the bridge on the creek bank, Kit? Jim and Allie May and I called that our tree, and had all sorts of adventures in and under it. We had a swing there and a crow's nest built in its branches. When you can walk without that crutch, we'll go down and see it."

"Oh, goody! And I want to go see the little lady in the brown house, too. May I?"

"Yes, when you outgrow your crutch."

"I'm going to try now,"

"No! Don't you dare!" cried Virginia in alarm.

"Well, I won't if you say No. But I'm getting pretty tired of it, and some day I might forget."

"You heard me, Katherine Martin! I said 'Don't you dare.' And I meant it!"

Kit laughed in answer, but exclaimed suddenly, "There's a car stopping at our lane. And its not the mailman. Oh, it's Mr. Barrett. What does *he* want. We didn't send for him to help us about anything."

"Hush, dear. He has a right to come. Maybe he has some business to talk about." Virginia quieted Kit as Mr. Barrett drew near.

The visitor was obviously embarrassed as he halted at the step. But Virginia gave him a reassuring smile.

"I suspect that you think I'm a fearful nuisance," he said. "But I'm in a quandary, and am coming to you for help. My young cousin arrived unexpectedly and wants to stay a week or so. I haven't any place to put her. I have just one small room myself. I could send her to Aunt Molly, but she has guests and her little house is full to capacity. Could you *possibly* take a roomer for a few days?"

"I'd be delighted to do anything I can to help you. But are the upstairs rooms fit for occupancy? I haven't been up."

"Oh, yes. I haven't been in them myself, but Aunt Molly said it made her homesick for the old days when she cleaned them, for they were just as your Grandpa left them. If you could let Sherry use one (she can eat down in the village or she is well able to pay her board here), it would be a tremendous load off my mind. She can't go right back home."

It flashed upon Virginia that another girl in the house would be a comfort as the dark drew on tonight—even if that girl were only a high-school freshman. She hoped her voice didn't sound too eager as she spoke.

"I'd be *so* glad to have her. Is she with you? Won't you bring her in?"

"Yes," he confessed sheepishly. "I did bring her with me. I

felt quite sure you'd do it. The Martins always did things like that."

He started down the lane toward the car, and Virginia remarked in a low tone to Kit, "Life brings some queer things to us, Kitten. In all my day dreams, I never once saw myself as the keeper of a rooming house."

"I hope she's a nice roomer. And I hope she's a *young* cousin. I need somebody to play with. And I *sure* hope she's better-looking than he is."

"Don't you like his looks?"

"Oh, so-so. He's O.K.—for a man. But a woman should be beautifuler."

They stood watching from the porch, and evidently the girl in the car interpreted their actions as consent, for she slid into the driver's seat, turned the car into the lane and came on at a breakneck speed, waving pertly at Steve Barrett as she passed him, then stopping at the steps with a squeal of brakes.

Kit was giggling at the trick, and even Virginia smiled as the newcomer sat and laughed at her cousin as he trudged back.

"For that trick," he grumbled as he stopped at her side, "I should let you sleep in a tree tonight. Miss Virginia and Miss Kit, this is my cousin, Sherry Carlson, and after this exhibition of her character I won't blame you if you refuse to let her enter your home."

Virginia's first thought was that Kit would be disappointed in all her expectations, for the tall thin girl who was pulling her suitcase from the back seat did not look as if she would satisfy anyone's desire for beauty. But when she extended her hand to meet their welcoming ones, she smiled and Virginia thought quickly, *Why, she's beautiful—she's lovely!*

"You mustn't make her sleep in a tree!" cried Kit. "I like her. I want her to stay here."

They went into the house and Kit led the guest hospitably to a chair.

"There's lots of room here," she said, as if fearful that

Sherry would not stay. "If there aren't any beds upstairs you could sleep on this davenport."

"That's not a davenport—that's a sofa," said Sherry, smiling at the little girl. "And if I slept there I'd have to pleat me like an accordion."

"I'll go and inspect the upstairs now," said Virginia, glad for the opportunity to make the inspection while a man was at hand to accompany her.

Reassured by his presence, she led the way up the narrow, walled-in stairway. There were three bedrooms with low, sloping ceilings and short, many-paned windows. Virginia took this opportunity to observe that every one of these windows was nailed shut, and that no one could have entered them last night. Tonight she would be sure that the door of the kitchen entry, and the one at the foot of the back stairs, were both tightly locked!

"There is space and equipment enough here for you to start in the hotel business," said Mr. Barrett. "I'm sure Sherry will be happy in any one of these rooms. I think she will be here for a short time only, until I can get her—some business transacted."

"Don't you think this room will be best? It is over the dining room and this register in the floor will let up enough heat for this moderate weather."

"Yes, yes! It will be fine. Miss Sherry should be very comfortable here."

His tone implied, thought Virginia, that Miss Sherry had better be comfortable or her cousin would wash his hands of her. Was she a problem child whose escapades were embarrassing to this serious-minded relative?

When they returned to the dining room, however, there were no problems in evidence. Kit and Sherry were side by side on the sofa, deep in examination of one of the precious scrapbooks that were the pride of Kit's life. It was one devoted to pictures of dogs, and the girls were fascinated by the canines that stared at them from every page. Evidently two dog lovers had met and formed a friendship.

"Sherry, there's a cozy little room upstairs, waiting for you. I hope you can understand how fortunate you are that Miss Virginia will take you in. She didn't have to, you know," Steve added rather sternly.

There was a sly twinkle in Sherry's eye as he said that and the corner of her mouth twitched as if she wanted to smile. But she only said, "You're a dear, Stevie. I really didn't want to sleep in a tree."

She followed him to the door when he left, and Virginia, from the other side of the room, heard him say, "I've done my best for you. Try behaving for this once, won't you?" Then in a sudden change of tone, "Keep a stiff upper lip, youngun. Things will work out O.K., I'm sure."

Chapter Seven

After Kit had retired that night, Virginia told Sherry about the happenings of the night before. They had insisted that she take supper with them and had enjoyed the further acquaintance that this fellowship brought. Now the two older girls were on the sofa in the dining room. Virginia was knitting, and Sherry was sitting idly opposite her, with her long legs curled under her and her hands clasped boyishly behind her head.

"Maybe you didn't really hear anything," she suggested. "You were nervous and imagined things. I don't believe that anything bad could happen in this sleepy little place."

"It might not have been anyone with harmful purpose. Maybe that girl was hitchhiking across the country, or something like that. She didn't look *bad*. She was startled like myself. She probably thought this was an empty house. Maybe it was nothing that could harm us, but I know it was *something*. I wouldn't dream up hot lamp chimneys and unwashed bowls. And my imagination wouldn't drink milk!"

Sherry laughed. "Well, hardly. Whoever it was is probably ashamed and sorry now, and I'm not afraid, are you?"

"No, not at all with you here. But I confess I'm very glad that you are here. If you don't want to sleep upstairs alone, you can have the sofa as Kit suggested."

"Phooy! I'm really not afraid."

Later in bed, Virginia lay relaxed and restful, calmed by the assurance that there was another young woman in the house. She even gave pitying thought to the strange girl of the hall mirror, hoping that wherever she might be tonight she might feel as secure and protected as Virginia did at this minute. Surely the coming of Sherry Carlson was a token of God's loving care for them. By the time she would have to leave them they would be at home in the old farmhouse and its corners would hold no fears.

At the breakfast table next morning Kit suggested that Sherry eat all her meals with them, and Virginia quickly seconded such an idea. In these days of loneliness to have such a lively companion as Sherry would be a blessing indeed.

"It's kind of you to want me," she said, "after the unceremonious way I was dropped in your lap. Cousin Steve is kindness itself, but no one ever accused him of knowing anything about the fine art of—of finesse. Is that redundant, teacher?"

"How did you know that I'm a teacher?"

"A bird told me—a six-foot bird who is inclined to stutter in the presence of beautiful ladies."

"Oh, you mean Mr. Barrett," said Kit. "I wouldn't call him a bird. He doesn't look like a bird. He'd be too solid to *ever* fly."

"Howsoe'er that be, Miss Kit-kat, I'll be glad to share meals with you for a few days. I can pay my way, I'm not a half bad cook, and as a scrub lady I'm unexcelled. I'll try not to shirk my share of the work."

She kept her promise and attacked vigorously any task that needed attention. She stayed with Kit while Virginia shopped or took long exploratory walks through the village or over the country roads. She read aloud during the evenings while Kit cut and pasted and Virginia knitted. On such evenings Mr. Barrett was apt to drop in to consult Sherry about some business that appeared to be troubling them and over which they held long and, often, heated discussions in the parlor with the door closed. Often he would remain to share the evening's fun. After a few visits he became 'Steve' to Virginia and Kit, and it was hard to realize that a very short time ago he had been an utter stranger to them. Now he seemed like a brother—one on whom they could rely if life became difficult.

After a week had gone, Virginia began to wonder how long the 'several days' would last, and to dread the time when Sherry's business might be finished. Kit, too, worried about such an eventuality, and one night when the pain in her leg had been unusually severe and Sherry had been rubbing it, she broached the subject.

"Sherry, why can't you stay with us always? I mean, as long as Ginny and I live here. We really *need* you."

Sherry laughed as she answered. "Thanks, ladybird, for the invitation and the inference that I'm helpful. But I'd be ashamed to stay. I haven't any excuse for being here as long as I have now."

"You don't need an excuse for staying. You need one for going. You don't really truly have to go, do you?" Kit's voice was anxious.

"Oh, Kit!" reproached Virginia. "Perhaps her folks want her to come home. We have no right to demand that she stay, just because we are enjoying her so much. After all, she only came on a visit, and may have other plans."

"It isn't that," said Sherry in embarrassment. "There isn't anyone who wants me. Steve is the only person I would consider. I don't think he cares where I stay, but I promised him I wouldn't go without letting him know about it."

"Haven't you *any* family?" asked Kit, aghast at such disclosures. "Doesn't anybody live with you?"

"Steve is the only person who cares what happens to me. He is a pain in the neck sometimes, but he's a grand chap and I intend to keep my word to him."

Virginia spoke hesitantly, but very earnestly. "I'm sorry, Sherry. Forgive Kit's inquisitive questions. If you *would* stay with us we'd be very happy. You've been so jolly and helpful that we'd miss you terribly. I don't see how we'd get along without you. So if you *could* stay, and want to, we—"

"Do you honestly mean that?"

"Of course I do. This house is so big that we need you to help fill it. Kit and I would rattle around in it if we were all alone. You have carried more than your share of the work and expense. We don't want to overpersuade you, but—"

"We just want you awfully," cried Kit. "I want you so badly that I know I'll have a dreadful fever if you go."

"I don't know what Steve will think of it. He's been in a stew about imposing on you by sending me here. He's trying to make some other plans for me, but I like this better than any other place. I've begun to feel as if I have a couple of sisters, and I'd hate to leave you when I just found you."

"I'll talk to Steve about it," said Kit importantly. "He does as I tell him."

This statement proved true. Kit's charm had won Steve's heart, and he was her willing and often overworked slave. He seemed relieved to have Sherry settled with them for a few weeks, though uncertain whether her presence was an advantage and joy to Virginia.

"I'm very glad for Sherry," he said to Virginia one day when he met her in the village and insisted on taking her and her load of groceries home in his car. "And in a way, I'm glad for you. I had a letter from your brother yesterday and he was a bit concerned about your isolation. The presence of Sherry will relieve him. But I can't feel that she can be much of an inspiration or bringer-of-joy in the home. Her disposition is so—so—well, to put it kindly, uncertain. There have been times in the last week when I have wondered how anyone could live with her. I don't blame—" He shrugged his shoulders, looked embarrassed as if he had said too much, then changed the subject and spoke of another matter that Jim had written about.

"Your brother has conceived the idea that we should institute a more vigorous search for your cousin, Allie May. He knows that your father was worried about it and believes that if we could find her it would do much to relieve his mind, so I'm going over all the papers thoroughly again to see if there is a starting place for investigation; then I'll get to work with renewed effort."

"That's a grand idea! If we could find even a trace of her, just enough to encourage Dad to feel that she would be found someday, it would be a tonic for him; that is," she added sadly, "if he ever wakes up and knows what is happening." Her chin quivered as she spoke, for the news from Mother had not been encouraging lately, and there had been dark hours during the nights when she lay awake at Kit's side.

"I'm sorry. I wish there were something I could do to help."

"You do—you've helped wonderfully. I don't know how Kit and I could have managed at all without you. You've done everything—from teaching me how to prime a pump to providing Sherry to help in our loneliness. I'm not usually despondent, but when I think of Mother down there alone, with Dad lying so helpless and unknowing, it—it—gets me down."

"I know. Would it help to know I'm praying with you?"

She looked up at him in surprise. They had stopped at the entrance to the lane so that Virginia might get the mail from the box, and Steve had not started the car again. Perhaps he felt that he did not want to bring this conversation, his first with Virginia alone, to an end. It was definitely not the kind of conversation that could be carried on in the presence of Kit and Sherry. Virginia made answer now in a voice that had more emotion in it than she cared to display.

"Would it help? Indeed it would! But why should you? I never had a friend who did that for me."

"Let me be your first prayer partner, then. Aunt Molly taught me that there is great blessing in praying for each other."

"You're wonderfully kind. I'd like to meet your Aunt Molly."

"You will in a day or two. She's away now. That boy who delivers your milk is the son of her neighbor who is caring for her place while she is gone. But she'll be back soon, and will appear at your back door with an inquiry as to whether she can be of help to you. She was a friend and neighbor of your grandparents, and will feel it a privilege to be neighborly to you."

He turned the car into the lane and waved at Kit who was watching them from the window. As they drew up to the porch Virginia spoke earnestly.

"I have much for which to thank you. Not the least of these things is Sherry. She isn't difficult—not often, anyway—when you aren't here. I think she likes to tease you. She's fine for Kit, and we both love her. Please believe that we want her and don't worry any more. Something tells me she's going to be a real blessing to the Martins."

This prediction proved true. She was more adept than Virginia at housekeeping. She knew the mysterious ways of coal fires and pumps. She professed to like dishwashing, which statement Kit doubted, but, most important, she did more for Kit's morale than anyone else had been able to do. She liked to play games and work on the scrapbooks, thus enabling Virginia to escape from the house in those hours when frustration and disappointment swept over her like a flood.

After the first excitement of moving and getting settled was over, those black moods were more frequent than she cared to let anyone know. Each day seemed like the one before it, with nothing accomplished except the round of household tasks. If she had possessed a talent for writing or drawing, she could have filled many dull hours and perhaps produced something that would, in a small measure, satisfy her yearning to contribute to the betterment of the world, something that would keep her name alive, but she had no such talent. She could not even sketch the old tree by the creek. As for writing, even her letters were hard labor. The only thing she liked to do, the only thing she could do well, was to teach. And that was denied her. The thought of this loss brought the realization of all that it entailed, and despair engulfed her.

It was at such times as this that she went for long walks alone. Usually it was a letter that started the train of thought that sent her forth thus. Jim's letters were newsy and frank, and when he met Howard Willis with Virginia's former associate in the English department he not only mentioned it but rejoiced over it. Jim had always termed Howard Willis a 'foul ball.' Letters from the other teachers confirmed this news, though of course they did not show Jim's elation over it.

"Better quit rusticating and come home to guard your property," wrote one of them. Virginia winced at that, though her lip curled a bit in scorn. She didn't want property that she had to guard. But, oh, how she did want Howard Willis not to be that kind of man!

The second Sunday that they were in the farmhouse, Sherry suggested that, if Virginia wanted to go to church, she would be glad to care for Kit.

"Oh, I'd like to. When Kit exchanges that crutch for a cane, I hope I can plan some way to get her there. It will be good to be back in church. But I don't want to be selfish. Maybe you'd like to go."

"Don't make me laugh. I love church like Kit loves her cod-liver oil. No, you go, and let me feel virtuous for staying with Kit."

She spoke bitterly, and Virginia was troubled by her attitude, but one didn't question Sherry on her whims and opinions so she said merely, "I think I'll go in time for Sunday school. It will seem more like a real Sunday if I do that. If there are any papers given out, I'll bring you one, Kitty."

The little brick church would not have housed one department of the Sunday school back home. The children pouring into the basement doors told her that the younger classes met down there. She went past them into the auditorium where all those of high-school age and older were meeting. As she spied a group of girls in one corner she found herself hoping that their teacher would be absent today and that she would be asked to teach them. But a young woman approaching them was greeted so enthusiastically that hope faded. In another corner Steve Barrett sat with a half-dozen boys. He gave her a smile of welcome which sent a warm glow through her heart. She wasn't entirely a stranger!

As she waited for the opening exercises to start she looked about her at the rows of seats curved in a semicircle facing the pulpit, at the short straight benches at the side of the piano—they were for the choir, she presumed, but were now occupied by the men's class—and at the stained-glass windows at either side. She remembered those windows. She looked across at the seat, second from the front on the side by the baptistry, where Grandpa had always sat. She and Allie May would be on one side of him and Jim on the other. Grandpa was wise enough in the ways of his youngsters to keep Jim and Allie May separated during church services. She and Allie May used to gaze at the windows and thrill at the colors when the sun shone through them. She noticed something now that she had not remembered. On the window that depicted the sower was an inscription, "To the memory of Joseph Henry Martin." Grandpa must have given that window, for Joseph Henry Martin was Dad's father, Grandpa's only son, who had died before Dad and Uncle Fred could remember. She had never thought of him, but now it seemed pathetic to her that he had lived and died and that even his sons could not remember him. Only a stained-glass window—a cheap stained-glass window—remained to remind the world of his existence. That was what life was like. Unless a person could leave behind some notable achievement he might well have never been born. The prospects were that Virginia Martin would join those whose generation bore no imprint of their work or character.

Virginia Martin also lived, she thought wryly.

She was aroused from her reverie by Steve's voice at her side. He asked anxiously, "You can play the piano, can't you, Virginia? Our regular pianist is ill, and her substitute cut her hand badly this morning. We haven't anyone else who can play at all."

She gave him a smile of happiness. "Indeed I can. I have been sitting here feeling sorry for myself, and the touch of a piano would be good medicine for me." This would be even better than teaching a class.

When the song service was ended and the group was breaking up into clases, Steve brought a kind-faced man to her and introduced him as the pastor, Mr. Davenport. The minister shook her hand warmly, saying with a note of apology in his voice, "Miss Martin, I conduct my own choir and I can tell that you're a capable pianist. We're in a bad spot this morning, as Steve has probably told you. Will you help us?"

"Gladly, if it isn't too difficult. I haven't practiced for weeks. I am substitute organist for my home church and I may be familiar with your selections."

"They aren't hard. Our choir is small and the voices not well trained. But we manage to make a joyful noise to the Lord."

Virginia was familiar with the score of the anthem, and found it easy to follow Mr. Davenport's direction. She thought she had never enjoyed an anthem so thoroughly. What the choir lacked in training it made up in spirit. The alto was a bit too strong for the sweet but thin soprano of the two young girls, and Steve's bass was not of the highest quality, but when Mr. Davenport himself sang the tenor solo, Virginia drew a breath of delight. Here was a real voice!

When the choir came down in preparation for the sermon, Steve saw to it that she sat by him. She was glad, for this gave her a feeling of belonging, and helped to beat back the homesickness that had been threatening her.

Driving her home after the close of the service, Steve asked hesitantly, almost as if he feared her answer, "How did you like us? I hope we didn't appear too uncouth."

"Of course you didn't. I liked every minute of it."

"Even having to play at a minute's notice?"

"That most of all. I've been homesick for my piano. That old organ of Grandpa's may have been a fine instrument in its day, but it has long passed that day."

He laughed, then said admiringly, "You can really play, and I don't mean maybe! Mr. Davenport gave us a pretty good sermon, too, didn't he? At least it seemed so to me." He added this last rather hesitantly, as if he feared that she, with her city-bred standards, might not rate Mr. Davenport and his sermon as highly as he did.

But she quickly put him at ease by saying, "I don't know whether it was a good sermon or not, but it did me a lot of good. It gave me much food for thought, and I'm going to have a better day and week, in spite of the 'thorns that prick and sting,' because of that sermon."

"I guess that's about the highest praise one could give a sermon. Its measure of worth should be its adequacy for human needs."

They drew up at the steps and she urged him to come in for Sunday dinner.

"Sherry is cook today, so it'll be good."

"Not for me, I fear. We had a slight difference of opinion when she was in my office yesterday and she probably would enjoy putting cayenne in my soup. In spite of that I'd like to come, but I promised the Davenports I'd be back there in time for dinner. May I have a rain check for this invitation?"

"Indeed you may. Let's say for next Sunday."

"Will do. By the way, I hope you'll come and play for us again tonight."

"Surely, if you need me."

As she stopped for a moment on the porch to watch his car jolt down the lane, she felt a glow of happiness. Steve Barrett was just like an older brother—a real substitute for Jim.

Chapter Eight

October passed and the gray days of November heralded the approach of winter. Life in the farmhouse had settled into a routine that was livened by the presence and pranks of Sherry Carlson. She had a boundless energy that kept her active from early morning until night. Usually she wore an old plaid skirt and a shapeless green sweater that was extremely unbecoming to her sallow complexion. Her dark hair was held back from her face with two large combs and twisted into a knot on top of her head. This added to her unusual height and made her look even thinner than she was. Virginia had a feeling that, because of her unhappy disposition, she was trying to look as unattractive as possible. Yet when she smiled there was an actual beauty in her thin face. She helped with the work, entertained Kit and planned jokes on Virginia and Steve.

But even Sherry's jokes and laughter could not make anything but drudgery out of the heavy tasks that confronted the girls every day. Having set her hand to the plow, Virginia had no thought of turning back, and because she did well anything that she did at all, her best effort was given to making a home for herself and Kit and to keeping the little girl well in body and happy in spirit. If she found it difficult to adapt herself to cooking on a coal stove, reading by a kerosene lamp and bathing in a tin tub in her bedroom, she kept her dislike to herself, and Kit continued to consider it all a great game which Ginny had invented for her enjoyment. Kit's health was improving and she greeted each new day with zest. So Virginia, remembering the listless, whining child that she had been six weeks before, struggled valiantly with the stove, polished lamp chimneys until they shone, and carried countless pails of water to the improvised bathtub.

Sherry and Kit, laughing at their games, never knew how often Virginia's heart was heavy with dread over the future or disappointment at the reports coming from the city, for Virginia's substitute was doing excellent work and the prevailing opinion was that she would fill the vacancy at the head of the department. Virginia knew the woman and her work and that it was entirely different from her own plans and purposes for the same position. If Miss Terrant had charge of the English department of Claremont High School, Virginia Martin would never fit in there again. She had a feeling of having been displaced already and forgotten. She was stranded here, and life was flowing past her, and she might never be able to launch into the stream again. Her work and her friend were taken from her. She knew now that Howard Willis had dropped forever from her life, for he had not written, and every report from the city told that he was not grieving over her absence. She tried to assure herself that his friendship was not worth a heartache if it meant so little to him, but it seemed unfair that this loss should be added to the other. She had been willing to make her sacrifice and had tried to accept it without visible rebellion, but she had not been able to anticipate all the heartaches that the days would bring. Her conflict was not a great battle that won a war. It was a day-by-day struggle.

There was another cause for heart-heaviness that she had to keep from Kit. Mother's letters had been bravely cheerful and the children had hoped that Dad might be brought home by Thanksgiving. Then the hopes were set ahead to Christmas. But when Mr. Hudson returned in mid-November from a trip to Mexico, he soberly told Jim that things were not going well in the little mission hospital. Dad's body was healing as well as could be expected, but he had not yet recognized Mother nor spoken a word since the accident. The doctors in charge could discover no reason for the condition, and unless there was a change soon they must get him to a larger hospital. Mr. Hudson wanted him taken to New York, but the risk would be great and the results of an operation might not be what they hoped. Jim called by telephone one night after Kit was asleep and said that both he and Mr. Hudson felt it was imperative that the trip be made. It might not be successful, but they must make every effort.

"It's only a chance, Ginny, but it's the only chance we have to get back our dad as he used to be," said Jim, with a break in his voice. "Shall we tell Mother we think it's the best thing to do?"

She agreed and they both wrote, but it was a hard task. Virginia had to word her letters carefully so that Mother would not realize that she was not still teaching. It could not disturb Dad, for nothing penetrated his slumber, but it might add to Mother's sorrow, so the letter was filled with assurances of their well-being, and their confidence in the decision to move Dad to New York as soon as possible.

After she had written the letter she walked down the lane to the mailbox. There was no hurry about the letter for the postman would not pass until nine-thirty tomorrow. But she felt that she must gain composure before going into the bedroom where Kit was sleeping. By the side of the lane was an old bench under a walnut tree. She remembered how Grandpa Martin had, in the long-ago days, sat there after the evening's work was done, and how she and Jim and Allie May had romped around him and played hide-and-seek in the orchard behind him. She sat in that beloved spot now and leaned her head against the rough trunk of the tree. She did not cry. Crying had never been a balm to her spirit or a relief when emotions swept her. Grampa had said once, "Martins don't cry!", and in that respect she was a true Martin.

But even though tearless, she felt shaken and forlorn. Was

this the way God wanted her to go? If so, why was the road made so difficult? She was so tired, so weary of planning to no purpose, so sick with foreboding for the future, that all strength seemed to have fled. Could she ever go back to the house and pick up the responsibility for Kit's care and the need for such decisions as she and Jim had made to-night? If Dad *never* recognized them again, could she face life at all?

She heard the car stop by the gate and the soft whistle that she recognized as Steve's, as he came toward her. When he saw her he stopped with a start.

"Why—hello! Who is it? Virginia? What are you doing here in the dark?"

She sat up and answered in a not too steady voice, "Gloomin', our colored laundress would have called it."

"Oh, that's not good. Is it bad news from home, or has Sherry been tormenting you?"

He sat down by her side as she answered his last question hastily. "No, indeed. Sherry is a dear!"

He grunted skeptically, but she went on. "I'd *die* here alone without her now. I can't tell you how much she has helped. No, I wasn't worrying about Sherry. It *was* bad news from home, and I don't want to go to bed until I've gotten on top of it. If I'm restless, it disturbs Kit, and I don't want her to know."

"Can I help? Is it anything the old family lawyer should know?"

She told him, and in spite of the Martin stoicism her voice betrayed her pain and fear.

"That's too big a load for one young lady to carry alone. I'm glad you told me. That's what friends are for—to help carry loads. I'm here to give anything I can in the way of assurance and comfort. And I can do more than that. I can pray. Will it help any to know I'm doing that?"

"Oh, it will! You depend much on prayer, don't you?"

"Let's say I depend much on the One to whom I pray; that is, I am learning to depend on Him. Until recently my Christianity has been more theoretical than clinical. But I've been trying to go a bit deeper into it lately and I'm finding the blessing of prayer."

"I'm glad to hear you say that. I need such assurance now as I never needed it. I've been wondering if prayer really does help things. I've never had any big problems before, at least none which compared with my present ones, and I've taken prayer as a formal act of worship rather than a means of help."

"Sure, it's a help. You ask Aunt Molly. She knows. It is she who has been helping me. She got back from her nephew's yesterday and will probably be up with your milk tomorrow. She has been through a hard school and learned her lessons by deep experience. She will be a bit quiet at first for she is a retiring soul, but when she becomes well acquainted you will find her a rare character."

"Perhaps she *can* help me. I've been troubled, because I want to be in God's will and to accept His leading, but it is hard when the way is so dark before me. I thought in August that everything was going to be right. Then after I had asked God to lead me and show His will for me, everything went wrong."

She told him of the consecration service in the home church, of the pledge she had made that night, and how difficult it was to accept the leading given her. He listened intently, then spoke abruptly.

"I must see Sherry on business for a few minutes. Then I'll ask her to keep an eye on Kit, and you and I will go for a ride. It's just the night for the open road. O. K?"

"O. K."

"Is that coat warm enough? Do you want a hat? Can Sherry give me one?"

"The coat is very warm and I have a scarf in my pocket. Tell Sherry to leave the bedroom door open so that she can hear Kit."

"I'll be back in a few minutes and then we'll head for the hard road and I'll show you what this antique bus can do."

At first, as they rode along the moonlit roads they did not talk. Virginia was so tired that she wanted only to relax and breathe deeply of the tangy autumn air. Mile after mile sped past, and the night with its mystery of scents and sounds began to have its effect on her. The load rolled off her shoulders and she felt renewed in faith and courage. Life was good in spite of the hard things. Kit was better, definitely so, and Dad would soon be in New York where the world's best surgeons could find his trouble and correct it. She did not even think of Claremont High School. Tomorrow that pain might return, but for tonight it had been forgotten. She drew a long breath of rested enjoyment. At her side Steve spoke at last.

"Well, that sounds better. Nerves all relaxed and un-knotted? There's nothing like the outdoors to do it, is there?"

"You're right. This is just what I needed. I *was* all tied in knots, I guess. This job I have now isn't the easiest one in the world and by night I'm really tired. The bad news about Dad tonight just about finished me."

"I'm sorry about that. But we're going to pray and be-lieve that it's going to be all right."

"It's so comforting to have a Christian friend. I don't know what I'd do without you and the little church. I wish Sherry were interested in going occasionally. We could take turns, and it would help her. I don't think she's very happy."

"No pagans are happy, and Sherry is a complete pagan."

"What a terrible thing to say! What do you mean?"

"Exactly what I said. She is a heathen. Isn't a heathen an uncivilized person who does not believe in God? Well, that's Sherry. She is both uncivilized and irreligious."

"But why? She is so nice in most ways. Kit and I love her."

"I'm ashamed to confess that I have a soft spot in my heart for her. There's something about her that—oh, it just gets you! But I heartily disapprove of her."

"I can't understand why—"

"No one understands any of the why's about Sherry Carlson. If I knew the reasons for her quirks of character I'd try to do something about them. She has made me more trouble than all my other clients put together, even counting the elusive Allie May Martin! I feel guilty at having wished her onto you, but I didn't know what else to do. But I'm afraid she'll have a bad effect on Kit. When she gets angry she's a terror, and if she decides to throw a real temper, you'd better call for me. I can take care of her."

"I'm glad that she has a cousin like you to take care of her. It's hard for a young girl to be so alone in the world."

"Alone? My eye! She isn't alone. She has a perfectly good family and home if she would only behave herself and go back to them. Did she tell you she was alone in the world?"

"Why—I can't remember. Maybe I just inferred it. She said that no one except you cared what she did—and I supposed she was an orphan."

Steve waited to answer until Virginia began to wonder if her curiosity had offended him. At last he spoke slowly.

"I can't tell you just what Sherry's trouble is. I don't know it all myself. I only know that she had a violent quarrel with her folks and came here looking for some place to stay. I took her in because I thought it better that she be here where I could keep an eye on her. I've been trying to patch it up but I haven't succeeded. I can't even find out what it's all about. I went up to her home last week, but it was no use. They don't know that she's here, but I told them she kept in touch with me. And I promised them I'd let them know if she needed anything. She doesn't— except for a sound spanking. You can't know how relieved I am to have her with someone like you. But I do feel ashamed to burden you. If she becomes a nuisance, you'll let me know, won't you? I'll send for Uncle Carl and Don and they can take her home in handcuffs."

"Oh, don't do that. When she goes she must go of her

own volition. That all explains why she is so unhappy. I don't mean that she is gloomy or irritable. She isn't, a bit. She's lots of fun. When Kit gets fractious she can calm her more quickly than I can. But once in a while she gets restless and there's a sort of desperate look in her eyes that makes me sick. Then she puts on her wraps and goes off toward the woods. She will be gone several hours, but she always comes back in a good humor. I have known that something was troubling her, but when she was so secretive I could do nothing to help."

"I hope that it is her conscience that is troubled. The folks wouldn't talk about it, but anyone could see that they are a heart-sick trio. If they weren't all so devoted to her, they couldn't be so deeply hurt as they are. It's a mess. But don't let her worry you."

"She doesn't worry me. But I couldn't understand why she resented my reference to my faith."

"I can't answer that. Uncle Carl and Aunt Hulda are staunch Christians. I don't know much about Don and Sherry. I hadn't seen any of them since I was a very small boy, until I went up when Don was in college. Uncle Carl is my mother's brother, but she died when I was six and I never knew much about her people. Perhaps the kids picked up some queer ideas in college. Aunt Hulda wouldn't have any patience with any liberal tendencies they might develop. Perhaps that's the trouble. Sherry isn't blessed with an overdose of patience herself. They're both stubborn, and just can't live together."

"Well, I hope she'll stay with us as long as she won't go home. I really mean that. She's lovable, and we like her. Perhaps someday she'll tell me what makes her so unhappy and I can help her."

"I doubt if anyone can help her until she's willing to admit her faults and say 'I'm sorry' to those whom she's hurt."

"That's another thing to pray about. You pray for my family and I'll pray for yours. Do you know that verse that says something about 'helping together by prayer'? I think it's in the first chapter of Second Corinthians. I found it the other day after you had promised to pray with me. I marked it in my Bible so I'd remember it."

"I never noticed that verse. I must find it and mark it also."

On through the quiet night they drove. Overhead the moon played hide-and-seek with the clouds, reminding Virginia of evenings on the porch deck at home and bringing back the homesickness of the earlier part of the evening. Steve, sensing her change of mood drove in silence, letting the beauty of the night do for her what his words could not accomplish. She recalled the Psalm which was her pastor's favorite:

> When I consider thy heavens, the work of thy fingers,
> The moon and the stars, which thou hast ordained,
> What is man, that thou art mindful of him?
> And the son of man, that thou visitest him?

Steve was singing under his breath:

> Abide with me: fast falls the eventide;
> The darkness deepens; Lord, with me abide:
> When other helpers fail, and comforts flee,
> Help of the helpless, abide with me!

> Swift to its close ebbs out life's little day;
> Earth's joys grow dim, its glories pass away;
> Change and decay in all around I see:
> O Thou who changest not, abide with me!

"Oh, Thou who changest not!" That was what she needed: someone who did not change; someone who never failed; someone so all-powerful, so all-loving, so ever-present that she could simply let go and rest in Him. She joined Steve:

> I need thy presence ev'ry passing hour:
> What but Thy grace can foil the tempter's pow'r?
> Who like Thyself my guide and stay can be?
> Thro' cloud and sunshine, Oh abide with me!

When they had finished Steve said, "Nothing like the old hymns, is there?" and started another:

I need Thee ev'ry hour,
Most gracious Lord;
No tender voice like Thine
Can peace afford.

The car was turning into the lane when Virginia spoke at last. "You can't know what you've done for me tonight. I was in the depths when you came. Now everything is all right. I won't get so low again. I know that."

"Good! I want to thank you, too. This is the first time I ever took a young lady for a ride and had it turn into a hymn sing. But I liked it more than any ride I ever had. You're sure you won't gloom any more?"

Virginia laughed. "No. You've driven the glooms away. I feel wonderfully rested. I'll go to bed and pray awhile and go to sleep. I know I will."

"Good! I'll go home and do the same. And while I'm praying I'll thank God for my new friend—a girl who loves the Lord and wants His will for her life."

Chapter Nine

Tue to Steve's prediction, Aunt Molly Haley appeared at their door the next morning with the milk. As if eager to get acquainted with them she lingered to chat about the memories she had of Virginia's little-girl days and of the other Martins who had been her friends and neighbors for most of the years of her long life. After that first morning she always sat awhile in the old rocker by the dining-room window, and somehow it became a custom with the girls to bring to her their problems or difficulties. She started Kit on an "Irish chain" quilt. She gave cooking lessons to Virginia, and encouraged Sherry to hunt through the pile of magazines that had accumulated on the table and find material for several different scrapbooks that she was making. She had several other customers on her route, but eventually Sherry took over the other deliveries, so that Aunt Molly could rest longer in the old rocker. In a short time she seemed to be an indispensable part of their lives.

One gray day in December she had spent the morning teaching Virginia the secrets of baking "salt risin' bread." Then she had been persuaded to stay for lunch, and, later, to help Kit with the sweater she was knitting for the dog she hoped to acquire someday. Sherry was arguing with Kit about the impracticability of making a sweater for a non-existent dog.

"Why don't you knit a sweater for yourself? You surely need one more than the little dog that isn't there does.

Or knit it for one of your brothers. A man can always use one more sweater."

"There are perfectly good reasons for doing it this way," answered Kit defensively. "This is my first sweater and I don't want to make such a big one. And," looking at it critically, "I don't think Kurt or Jim would wear it. It looks funny in some spots."

"Give it to Steve, then. If you made it, it would be perfect in his eyes."

"I *want* to make it for my dog. I *know* I'll have one someday. Mother will buy me all the sweaters I need but I don't think she would buy a dog sweater even for my birthday."

"O.K. Have it your way. When it's done, I suppose you'll use it as an argument to prove that you need a dog."

Kit gave a gasp of pleasure. "That's a perfectly splendid idea, Sherry. I hadn't thought of that!"

Sherry laughed and went back to her clipping. In looking for the articles that Aunt Molly wanted she found so many other things to interest her that the magazines, when she had finished with them, had the appearance of having been the playthings of a destructive puppy. She had not decided what she would do with the poetry, pictures, recipes and other clippings, but she was saving them, "just in case," she said.

Virginia, at the other end of the table, was trying to reconcile her checkbook with the bank statement that had just come. This was a task that always required all her attention, for she was notably weak in mathematics, and her addition and subtraction were liable to produce some disastrous mistakes.

The afternoon was so dark that when they had finished lunch and settled to the afternoon's occupations, Virginia had already pulled down the shades and lit the lamps. None of them noticed the flight of time until Aunt Molly, looking up from the sweater in which she had been picking up dropped stitches for Kit, said in dismay "Why, it's almost ha' past four. My fire will be out and it's high time I was startin' the chores."

She started for her wraps, and Sherry rose to assist her. A sharp rap at the door startled them and when Virginia opened it they all exclaimed in amazement. The world outside was a whirling mass of snow so thick that the fence across the drive was invisible. As Steve came stamping in looking like an arctic explorer, Aunt Molly frantically struggled with her wraps.

"Oh, I *must* get on home. I didn't sense it was snowin' so hard!"

"No, you can't, Aunt Molly," remarked Steve. "You couldn't make it in this blizzard."

"But I *have* to," she cried in distress. "The milkin's to do and the chickens to feed!"

"Can't help it. You'd never make it. I'd be afraid to try to cross that pasture myself."

"Well, you ain't crossed it as many times as I have, young man. I'm goin' right *now*."

"No, Aunt Molly! I mean it. You can't."

"But the milkin'—"

"I'll call Ed Harnish. He'd only have to cross the road. He can milk for you."

Aunt Molly listened dubiously as he rang for her neighbor, but when Ed had answered and had agreed to milk the cows and feed the chickens, she became resigned to staying until the storm passed.

"Oh, goody!" squealed Kit. "Goody! Goody! We can have a house party. Steve will have to stay, too!"

"I'm half afraid you're right," he said ruefully. "I thought I'd never get here. But I couldn't turn around to go back, and I wanted to assure myself that your fuel supply was sufficient for a spell of bad weather."

"Did you ever hear of that little gadget called a telephone?" asked Sherry sarcastically.

"I wanted to see with my own eyes," he said defensively, with a blush deepening the red that the wind had put into his cheeks. "I didn't think you girls would realize what you're in for. If the coal pile is low, I can split some of those logs in the shed."

"I'm glad you won't have to," said Virginia appreciatively. "I had a load of coal delivered last week. So let the blizzard bliz!"

"That's what it's doing!" cried Kit from the window where she had her nose pressed to the pane. It's so funny out that I feel lonesome inside me. I'm glad you're all here. I'd feel queerer if Ginny and I were here alone."

"Where did you leave your car, Stevy?" asked Aunt Molly. "It'll be snowed under till we have to shovel it out."

"I drove it into the old machine shed, so it'll be O.K. If the snow quits soon, I may be able to get back to town. I have a shovel and can dig myself out of drifts. I don't mind it if I can see where I am going. But it kept getting worse as I came along, and the last few rods were pretty rugged. I wouldn't have been surprised to find myself in the creek. I was glad to see the old shed loom up."

They had an early supper, for the darkness outside made them feel that night had come even though the clock did not confirm the reaction. Then they gathered around the dining-room table. This room, shut in on three sides by the other rooms of the house, was the warmest place they could find. Only when they were close to the windows could they realize how furiously the wind was blowing and how fast the snow was drifting across the drive by the porch.

"I think this is *so* much fun!" cried Kit after a stay at the window where she had tried in vain to catch sight of some landmark amid the whirling snow. All she could see was the white wall that shut them in, and she turned back to the heat and light of the room.

"It's cozy to be all here together around the stove. I like stoves better than furnaces, anyway. They're *much* more friendlier."

"Oh, your grammar!" moaned Sherry. "But I agree with

your sentiments. I'm even glad Steve got here. It's comforting to have a man on hand if we have to be dug out."

Virginia smiled across the table at Steve and said, "I'm glad, too. You said you would be out today, and if you weren't here I'd be worried for fear that you were stuck in a drift somewhere."

"In that case he'll have to stay," said Sherry flippantly. "We can't have you lying awake all night worrying about him."

"I very nearly didn't get home in time to come out. My train was late at the Junction and I only caught the other by the tail as it pulled out. I am lucky not to be marooned in that little station tonight."

Sherry looked up inquisitively. "Where have *you* been on a train?"

"It's really none of your business, Miss Pry. But I'll tell you, anyway. I've been out on the trail of a certain Allie May Martin, and one swell chase she's given me."

"Are you really on her trail?" asked Virginia eagerly. "Have you found out something about her?"

"No. I should'nt have said that, for I haven't a thing that could help in the least. I went to a small town up north where some Ormands are living, but they've never heard of Neil Ormand. So I came home no wiser than when I went."

"I'm sorry," said Virginia. "I keep hoping that we can find even one little clue so that when Daddy comes home we can tell him. It would make him happier than anything else could, I believe."

"Why should he care so much?" asked Sherry in her abrupt way. "He hasn't seen her since she was a little girl, and he can't be very fond of her after all this time. You said that if she weren't found soon, the whole farm would go to him. If she doesn't want to make herself known to you I think you should let her alone. Then everybody would be happy!"

"Dad would never take it, and he'll never be real happy

until she's found. The whole affair has been the big heart-break of Dad's life. It was hard enough for him to lose his only brother, but to be separated from Uncle Fred's wife and child has hurt him terribly, too. Always when we've planned some treat or surprise for Dad we've wished that we might, instead, return Aunt Alice and Allie May to him."

"Can you remember what made them leave here? I've heard several tales of some trouble between Neil Ormand and your grandfather, but there isn't a thing in all the papers I have that tells the truth of the matter," said Steve.

"I never could get it straight what the fuss was all about, for I was only eight years old and the talk I heard had little meaning to me. And Dad would not talk to us about it. But it was something about some money. Aunt Alice took Allie May back to live with her parents, and then they all moved away from here. That winter Grandpa died. We've been hunting for Allie May ever since, be-cause half of this farm is hers. That's all I know."

"Well, if she doesn't want to be found, I'm on her side," said Sherry. "She's probably an unpleasant brat who doesn't deserve any sympathy, but I admire her spunk. I hope you never find her!"

"You're cross!" said Kit. "Why do you always act so bad when Steve is here? I don't know anything about Allie May, but if Daddy wants to find her, I hope he does."

Aunt Molly, who had been sewing on the Irish-chain quilt, looked up as if disturbed by the turn the con-versation had taken.

"She will be found I'm sure. I've asked the Father for that every day since she left, and He will answer. The money will be found, too. That's why she don't want to come back. She was bad hurt over that. Even as a little girl she took things hard. An' to lose her father an' be separated from her grandpa bothered her terrible. The Ormands was all so cut up over it that they'd teach her to feel that way, too. But God has give me confidence, and it'll come out right in His time."

Sherry's belligerence seemed to fade at these earnestly-spoken words, and Virginia drew a breath of relief. There were times when Sherry's strong opinions and Kit's quick reactions rasped on her nerves, already worn thin by the weeks of strain she had undergone. She hoped some more pleasant topic of conversation would arise, but before anyone had a chance to change the subject Kit spoke eagerly.

"Oh, Aunt Molly, do you know about it? What money will be found? And why did Allie May feel so bad she won't come back?"

Aunt Molly glanced inquiringly at Steve as if she feared his disapproval, but he smiled encouragingly at her.

"Go on," he said. "It can't do any harm. The Kitten has as much right to know as anyone else. You don't mind if she tells about it, do you?" He looked inquiringly at Virginia, who promptly gave her assent.

"Yes, I do know as much about it as any livin' person," began Aunt Molly. "I was born and raised right in this valley and I knowed your folks all my life. I was right here when all the trouble started, and I done all I could to patch it up. But it wasn't any use, and then your grandpa died and nobody could find Alice and Allie May, and all I could do was to pray. I've been doin' that ever since. And someday I'll look up and see 'em comin' down the lane like they used to. That's the confidence I have."

"Tell about it. Tell *all* about it," urged Kit. "I don't know anything about any of the folks who used to live here, except stingy little dabs that Ginny and Jim let come my way once in a while. I was born too late! Go on and tell, *please!*"

Aunt Molly needed no urging, for the matter lay so close to her heart that she was eager to discuss it. So she began her story, while she stitched industriously at the quilt blocks.

Chapter Ten

Well, I was born in that little house I still live in. I never lived anywheres else. As far back as I can remember, Joe Martin lived on this farm. His only child was just my age and was always in my classes at school. We went to the little frame building that Bart Savage uses for a feed store now. They moved it up to his place when they built the new brick school the year Maw died. Joe Martin's son was named Joe, too, but we called him Jodie. When he was about ten years old the Ormands bought the house up yonder on the hill. They had just one son, too—he was named Neil—and from the first day they met at school, Jodie and Neil was friends. The teacher called 'em Damon and Pythias, but I always thought of 'em as David and Jonathan. Well, we all growed up and the boys was sent away to school. Neil went to business college in Sparta. His father said a farmer needed to know something about business as much as a banker did. He met Sadie Pace there and married her later. She belonged to the Paces over by the Junction. Jodie wanted to go to Sparta with Neil, but Joe had set his heart on sendin' him to college. Jodie was the only child Joe and Lydy had raised out of four or five children—I forget just how many they was—and they was determined he should have every chance. He kep' sayin' he didn't want to go to college at that ol' city, but wanted to go to Sparta. But Joe was firm and said he'd like it after he got started. I don't think he ever did like it or done

81

well with his books. All he wanted was to get back to the
farm and his paw and maw and Neil Ormand. But he
stuck to it cause he was a good boy. That last year in college
he met a girl. Her first name was Sue. I've plum forgot
the other one. Sherry woulda called her a glamour girl. Poor
Jodie thought she was the prettiest and the sweetest girl in
the world.

"They was married the day after he graduated an' he
brought her back to the farm with him. They stayed about
a month, as I recollect. Then she give him a choice between
her and the farm. Joe and Lydy was plenty disappointed,
but they didn't hold marriage light like folks do now an' they
knowed he had to go with her. Neil Ormand married an"
kept the farm after his folks died. He and Sadie had a
little girl named Alice. Joe Martin used to think the world
of that little tyke. Guess he was lonesome for Jodie's
babies. Jodie had two boys and once in a while he would
bring 'em and stay at the farm for a few days. Sue never
come at all. Jodie had a good job in the city, but he always
looked kinda peaked and unhappy. So Joe Martin grew to
lean more and more on Neil Ormand just like *he* was his
son."

Aunt Molly stopped for a moment to thread her needle.
Kit was listening in absorbed silence. Steve and Virginia had
laid aside their books and were giving full attention to this
story which held more interest for them than any romance
or travelogue. Sherry had discovered a fascinating serial in her
old magazines, and had withdrawn to the small table in the
corner as if the chronicle of the Martin family bored her.

"I was helpin' Dorry James that winter an' we didn't have
a telephone so I didn't know Jodie Martin was dead till
Paw come over one day an' said he was gone and Joe and
Lydy had the boys. Lee was four then an' Fred three—
just Alice Ormand's age. Joe said they had come for a
visit, but they never went back. Their mother married
again, and the Martins was tickled as could be when she
signed the boys over to Joe."

She stopped again, and Kit spoke impatiently. "But what about Allie May and the money? That's what you started to tell."

"I'll get there presently. I guess I do get to dwellin' too much on things that don't mean nothin' to you. But I'll hurry along. The children all growed up, and Lee married and moved to the city. He's your daddy now, Kit. Fred married Alice Ormand and they lived here with old Joe. Lydy was ailin' and Alice had to run the house. Lydy never had much heart left after Jodie died and fin'ly she took to bed. Can you remember her, Virginny?"

"Just a little. She lay in the big bed in the downstairs bedroom, and she would forget who I was."

"Yes, her mind failed toward the last. She was near eighty when she died, though. Fred and Alice had a little girl, Allie May, and she was the dearest treasure Joe Martin ever possessed. She was a lively youngun and the whole neighborhood was kept laughin' at her pranks. I guess we all get softhearted as we get older. Anyway, Joe Martin did. He loved all of his grandchildren, but his whole life seemed tied up in that child. They was together so much that she had his ways exactly, an' we used to say that Joe Martin would never die as long as that little girl lived. You remember her, don't you, Virginny? You an' your brother used to come out summers and the three of you were like wild Injuns."

"Yes, I remember her. I couldn't *ever* forget her. She meant more to me at that time than any other person in the world I think."

"Do you really remember her, Ginny?" squealed Kit. "I didn't know that. What did she look like?"

"Like a cocker spaniel." laughed Virginia.

Sherry raised he head from her story and gazed at Virginia in scorn. "How silly! No one ever looked like a cocker spaniel!"

"Well, Allie May did," said Virginia, nettled at Sherry's attitude. "Jim noticed it first. She had big brown eyes and a mop of dark hair that was always falling over her face. I can see yet the toss she would give to throw it back. Aunt Alice wanted to cut it but Grandpa wouldn't let her. Yes, she looked just like that. I thought her the most beautiful person in the world!"

Aunt Molly bit off a thread, then spoke reminiscently. "I always had a feelin' that she wasn't a girl at all but one of them pixie critters that hatched out of an acorn in the woods. She was—"

"A fawn, probably," interrupted Sherry. "I'm sure her ears were pointed."

"I don't know what you mean!" cried Kit. "But her ears must be burning now. I don't think it's nice to talk about her this way."

"It isn't," Virginia admitted. "Allie May has probably grown into a lovely woman. She was a charming child."

Kit looked soothed, but Sherry gave a wicked chuckle as she turned back to her reading.

"She's probably grown into a mastiff or a greyhound."

No one answered this sally and Aunt Molly continued. "I can remember her like it was yesterday. She and Old Joe was always together. She'd ride on the horse while he plowed or drive the team while he pitched hay. Neil Ormand was just as crazy about her and it's a wonder she wasn't ruint by all the attention she got."

"Guess she was about ten when the trouble come. Fred Martin hadn't been well all summer but help was hard to get and old Joe was gettin' pretty feeble, so Fred kept on goin'. He never had been real husky. Most of us thought he was a mite lazy. Didn't have half the get-up-and-go that his grandfather did. But that year he went hard to keep things going. One day he decided to walk over to Neil's to talk about sellin' a team of young horses. Thought he'd get a new car if he could get a good price for the team. Neil had always wanted them. Joe saw him go, from the garden where he was pickin' some beans for seed. About sundown he started to the house and there by the side of the shed was Fred, unconscious. They got him into the house, but he died that night without comin' to. He mumbled and talked some but it didn't make any sense and he didn't know any of us. I helped Alice and was here when he died. The doctor said his heart had been bad for a long time, but he hadn't told anybody but his brother Lee.

"Well, a couple of weeks went by, and one morning Neil Ormand come over after the horses. Said he had paid Fred five hundred dollars the day he died. Joe said they'd been no money on Fred when he got home. Everbody looked high and low for that money. Neil and Joe both got pretty excited. I never thought they meant to accuse each other. But Joe thought Neil was thinkin' that him or Fred had hid that money. And Neil felt Joe thought *he* was lyin'. They fin'ly had some terrible hard words over it. Alice and Allie May went over ever inch of the path through the field and pasture. They even waded out in the crick and looked for that money. Fred's wallet was gone, too, and Alice said she was sure the money was in it. Poor Alice nigh went crazy. The two men kept arguin', and fin'ly Alice took Allie May and went back to live with her paw and maw. And, come Thanksgivin' time, Neil sold his farm and moved away. He didn't tell any of his neighbors what he was doin', and was gone before we knowed it. Old Joe seemed to go all to pieces then. He got so quiet it scared us, and in February he died. His will, a new one he had signed up in January, said the farm was not to be sold till Allie May was found— that is, not unless they couldn't find her in twenty years. She was to get half of it and Lee and his children the other half. I think he realized how hurt Alice was for he acted like he knowed it would be hard to find her. That's how it stands now. The twenty years is slippin' past, an' if she ain't found soon the farm will have to go."

"Poor Allie May!" said Virginia. "I begin to remember more of it as you talk. Dad came down and talked to Aunt Alice and they both thought Uncle Fred had done something with that money when he began to feel sick. There had been two tramps hanging about the neighborhood and he may have feared that they would rob him while he was ill. Dad and Auntie looked every place they could think of—even the machine shed and the barns and the chicken house. But they couldn't find a thing. Dad tried to talk to Grandpa and Mr. Ormand about it and convince them that the tramps did rob Uncle Fred. Maybe that was what brought on the attack. But they were both so mad that they wouldn't listen. Then they all moved away and we haven't been able to find them."

"I think that's awful!" gulped Kit. "Of course Uncle Fred didn't do anything wrong, and I don't blame Allie May for feeling bad. She prob'ly just cried and cried! But I wish she would come back and take part of the farm and let us love her. I wish Aunt Alice would come with her,— and her grandpa and grandma, too. I want them *all* to come."

"I reckon Neil and Sadie are gone, by now. They'd be near eighty now, and Sadie hadn't been well since she got too hot once in threshin' time. But I'd sure like to see Alice again."

"I've wondered if Alice married again and the little girl took her stepfather's name. I'm going to put some ads in papers throughout the country promising a reward for any information about them," said Steve.

"If we could have just a clue before Dad comes home, I'd feel like a million dollars," Virginia sighed. "Think what it would mean to us all if we could write him a letter and say that we were on her track at last!"

Steve clapped his hand to his coat pocket. "Speaking of letters, here is one I was asked to deliver to you." He handed the letter in Sherry's direction, but she did not take it. Gazing back at Steve with flashing eyes she asked, "Have you broken your promise to me?"

"No, I've broken no promises," he said sternly. "But when I got this and was asked to send it to you, I was happy to do so, hoping you would be glad to receive it."

Twice she reached for the letter and drew back without touching it. She drew several deep breaths, and her whole body was shaking as if with a chill. The others in the room were silent as they watched the cousins facing each other, Steve pleading with his eyes and his outstretched hand, Sherry defiant. Even as they watched she burst forth.

"I don't care what they wrote to you, and I don't want any letters. Here's what I'll do with it!"

Before Steve had realized her intention she had jerked the missive from his hand and, raising the lid of the stove, had dropped it on the coals. Once her hand reached out as if to snatch it back, but it was blazing, and with a reckless laugh she replaced the lid and turned away.

Steve's face was white with anger, but he only said quietly, "Someday, Sherry Carlson, life will catch up with you and you'll learn that it doesn't pay to break hearts and then laugh about it."

"Life caught up with me so long ago that I've forgotten what it was like not to have a broken heart! As for Don and Mother and Dad, they have each other and that's all they need. They're utterly sufficient for each other."

Steve did not answer and the silence in the room grew embarrassing. Aunt Molly said softly, "It's gettin' on to ten o'clock. I always read a chapter from my Bible 'fore I go to bed. Do you want I should read out loud?"

"Oh, do!" said Virginia, feeling that before they could sleep something must clear the atmosphere.

Steve had sat down again, close to Aunt Molly's side. Virginia drew Kit's chair near to her own and nestled the little girl's head on her shoulder. Sherry turned away and went on with her reading. Aunt Molly opened the Bible and began to read:

> I will bless the Lord at all times:
> His praise shall continually be in my mouth.
> My soul shall make her boast in the Lord:
> The humble shall hear thereof, and be glad.
> O magnify the Lord with me,
> And let us exalt his name together.

> I sought the Lord, and He heard me,
> And delivered me from all my fears.

The words fell like soothing balm on the troubled hearts. Kit relaxed and listened like a tired baby. She forgot the pain that had increased as the cold grew more intense, and remembered only how warm and cozy it was here at Ginny's side. Steve felt ashamed of his anger at Sherry and resolved to be more patient with her and to try harder than ever to solve the difficulties in her life. Virginia forgot the discouraging news from Mexico and the vision of a pile of tumbled building blocks that had been bothering her all day, and let herself rest in the assurance of divine love and guidance. Sherry was absorbed in her magazine and gave no heed as Aunt Molly continued to read the Psalm:

> O taste and see that the Lord is good:
> Blessed is the man that trusteth in him.
> O fear the Lord, ye his saints:
> For there is no want to them that fear him.
> The young lions do lack, and suffer hunger:
> But they that seek the Lord shall not want any good thing.
> The righteous cry, and the Lord heareth,
> And delivereth them out of all their troubles.
> The Lord is nigh unto them that are of a broken heart;
> And saveth such as be of a contrite spirit.
> Many are the afflictions of the righteous:
> But the Lord delivereth him out of them all.
> The Lord redeemeth the soul of his servants:
> And none of them that trust in him shall be desolate.

Aunt Molly closed the Book and bowed her head above it. Her voice was that of a trusting child.

"Dear Father, we thank Thee tonight for Thy protecting care in the midst of this storm. We thank Thee that we are sheltered and warm. Give us restful sleep, Father, and let us wake up to another day of service for Thee. Help them who need Thee. Forgive them who err, and may we delight ourselves in Thee that we might be given the desires of our hearts. For Thy glory we ask it. Amen."

In the silence that followed, Virginia rose to prepare the beds.

"Sherry can sleep on the cot in our room, and Aunt Molly can have her room upstairs. It is as warm as toast, shut in as it is on three sides and with that great register in the floor. All those other rooms up there are too cold to be used, so I'll get blankets and a pillow for Steve and he can sleep on the davenport in the parlor. If this door is left open it won't be bad."

"It will be fine. I feel like a bum, coming in on you like this. But I had come too far to go back before I realized how bad it was. And I did want to get the letter to Sherry. A lot of good it did, though," he muttered under his breath.

After Kit was tucked in, and Aunt Mollie had gone upstairs, and Steve had retired to his bed in the parlor, Virginia went to the kitchen to fill the hot-water bottle. Kit's leg was aching and needed the soothing heat. Sherry followed her out and said, as they waited for the water to boil, "Aunt Molly's an old dear, and I wouldn't hurt her feelings by saying so, but I wish she'd keep her religion to herself. It gives me the willies!"

Virginia turned a shocked face to her. "Why, she isn't offensive about it. *I* like it. I certainly feel as if I can use all the strength and comfort I can get, and she really helped me tonight."

"That's just psychological. Her quiet tone soothed you and her faith inspired you. But that's all there is to it. She could have done as much for you by reading some beautiful poem."

"Why—why—don't you *believe* the Bible?"

"No! And I'll bet you don't either."

"I do, *too*. I always have. How can you *not* believe the Bible?"

"Because I think. And you believe because you don't think. You just jog along in the way you were taught and have never given any real consideration to it. You believe because your father and grandfather did."

"That's not so! My faith is my own. I believe because—"

"Oh, let's not argue. You believe that you believe, and I know I don't. And I don't want to. The water's hot. Let's go to bed."

The old house grew quiet. Outside, the storm raged. The drifts piled higher and higher, and the wind blew until the big maple tree by the porch groaned and creaked. Inside, the occupants snuggled into the warm blankets and let the wind lull them into dreamy thoughts. Aunt Molly hoped Ed Harnish had bedded the cow well, then thanked God for His care in the day just gone, and added a prayer for Allie May Martin. Kit hoped it was warm and comfortable where Mother and Daddy were, and planned the letter she would write to them tommorrow. Steve recalled the lonely years he had spent in a boardinghouse and thought how nice it was to be part of a family circle again, even if only as an uninvited guest. Virginia, lying quietly that she might not disturb Kit, mused on the conversation in the kitchen and grieved that anyone so dear as Sherry could be when she wanted to should avow herself openly an unbeliever. On the cot across the room Sherry pulled the covers over her head and sobbed into the pillow with longing for the letter she had burned. While a hundred miles away Don Carlson and his parents knelt and prayed with tear-wet eyes," Oh, God, keep our Sherry and bring her back to us and Thee."

Chapter Eleven

During the night Virginia heard Steve putting coal on the fire. *It must be a terribly cold night if he has to do that,* she thought. She was glad there was a man in the house to do it. Lying awake a while after that, she found her thoughts returning to Allie May. Wouldn't it be wonderful if they could find her before Dad got home? That is, if he ever did get home. She put that thought away and tried to picture how her cousin would look now. One thing was sure. She would be beautiful, like a dark-eyed little doll. She remembered that the ten-year-old Allie May had been smaller than eight-year-old Virginia. Yet the force of her personality had made her the leader of the Martin trio. Every game or plan had its roots in her fertile brain. And when they got into trouble—as they frequently did—it was her powers of persuasion that prevented the deserved punishment. She and Jim had had a childish love affair that last summer, and had planned to marry and live in the "crow's nest" in the big tree by the bridge. Virginia remembered how left out she had felt when she heard them planning to lower buckets to draw water up from the creek and to hang cradles on the branches to swing their babies to sleep. They wrote letters to each other and she never could find out where they hid them. Even now, Jim wouldn't tell. They had often talked since of what a lovable little minx Allie May had been.

Virginia drifted off into sleep again, to be wakened hours

later by Sherry and Kit calling to each other across the room.

"Look, Sherry! It's almost to the top of the window!"

"I'll say it is! No wonder it's so dark. I wonder if it's so deep everywhere, or is that just a drift?"

"Let's go see. We could. It's almost eight o'clock."

Virginia joined them and the three, in bathrobes and slippers, hurried out to the dining room. Here, also, was the strange gloom that made an eerie twilight in the daytime. Steve and Aunt Molly heard them and came in from the kitchen where Steve had biult a fire in the range.

"We're snowed in for sure," said Steve. "And there's more coming. There's a drift on the front porch that's so high a fat girl like Kit would get stuck between it and the roof!"

"I'm going to see."

But when they cautiously opened the door they looked in amazement at the sight that confronted them. A white wall reached almost the entire height of the door frame. Kit turned to Steve in consternation.

"Is it so deep on every side? How will we get out?"

"We won't get out. We'll have to stay in," said Virginia.

"Not on your life!" cried Sherry. "I'll go upstairs and climb out on the porch roof and take off from there."

"That might work with a long-legged shikepoke like you," conceded Steve. "But don't let Aunt Molly or Tubby here try it. They wouldn't be found till the spring thaws."

"Oh, for some snowshoes." Virginia sighed. "Kurt got some skis for Christmas last year and we had a lot of fun with them. If I had them, I'd go to Aunt Molly's barn and get some milk for breakfast."

"Well, you ain't got skis, nor yet snowshoes. I'll have to admit I wouldn't tackle crossin' that pastur' for love nor money. The drift in that hollow will be ten foot deep."

"There's still a quart of milk in the pantry," said Sherry, "so you won't have to sally forth in search of vittles yet a while."

"My, how funny to have the lamps lit at nine o'clock in

the morning!" exclaimed Kit as they gathered around the table to eat the bowls of oatmeal that Aunt Mollie was putting before them. "Isn't it queer how anything as white as snow is can make a house so dark? I wish I had two good legs and some snowshoes, and that Jack and Fran Fields were here. We'd have some fun! Oh, I don't like being a cripple!"

"Being a cripple doesn't make much difference this morning," said Virginia from her station at the front of the stove where she was making toast on forks before the open grate. "We're all snowed in together, and instead of thinking about winter sports we'd better be checking on our supplies."

"What's the matter, cook? Provisions low? If I'd known I was going to stay indefinitely, I could have brought some food."

"There's plenty to eat—of a sort. I bought a bushel of potatoes and one of apples from a farmer the other day. He said they'd keep fine in the cellar here. I didn't dream I was laying in supplies for a siege. I have plenty of sugar, flour, shortening and spices. But I have only seven eggs, no milk except in cans, and no fresh meat. There's lots of canned vegetables and tuna and salmon, so we won't starve. But if we stay here long we'll probably yearn for milk and meat!"

"You're a pretty good provider," commended Steve. "Having unexpected guests is apt to cause any hostess some anxious moments. Don't worry. As long as the potatoes and apples hold out we won't lose weight. And when the storm is over I'll give you a pantry shower that will leave you prepared for another blizzard!"

Hour after hour the snow continued to fall. The wind still blew a gale, but the snow, piled high around the old house, kept out the blasts, and the prisoners did not feel the bitter cold. That day seemed twice as long as a usual day. Virginia, saying that they must conserve kerosene, put out the lamps, so they sat around in the half-light, playing games that Sherry invented and making plans for the time when they could get out into the world again. Prompted by sheer boredom, they ate an early supper, then delayed their retiring lest they endure a sleepless night.

They were grouped around the one lamp on the dining-room table, Aunt Molly reading her Bible, Steve and Virginia playing checkers on the old board Steve had found in the parlor, Sherry and Kit working on the dog scrapbook. None of the young people had zest for their pursuits, for the inactivity of the day had wearied them of such pastimes. Sherry made frequent trips upstairs and looked out of the windows, hoping each time to report a diminishing of the snowfall.

"I never saw so much snow!" she said after one of these excursions. "Aunt Molly, did it *ever* snow so much as this before?"

"Oh, sure," answered the old lady. "About ever' ten year or so we have to have a storm like this. Guess God knows we need to stay in and think a few hours instead of rushin' 'round like mad. It gives us a chance to kinda get acquainted with ourselves if we have to stay home and be quiet a spell."

"I don't want to get acquainted with me, no more so than I am now. I know too much about me now. Further acquaintance would breed even greater contempt."

"That may be true for you, young lady, but some of the rest of us are not so fearful of a bit of introspection," said Steve, taking two of Virginia's men by a clever bit of strategy.

Sherry flipped a piece of paste-smeared paper in his direction, and both she and Kit giggled when it landed in his hair. Aunt Molly, as if sensing an incipient storm, hastened to remark, "Not that this ain't about the worst storm I ever saw. And it ain't through yet. It may be lots deeper than this 'fore it quits."

"Did you really ever see a bigger snow than this, Aunt Molly?" asked Kit, laying down the scissors and stretching her cramped fingers. "When was it? Were you shut in your little house all alone?"

"Well, the biggest snowfall I remember was when I was ten year old. That was an awful one. Yes, I was livin' in the same little house, but I wasn't alone, by any means. There was eight of us there that night. I never will forget it."

"Was there something special about it? Tell us, Aunt Molly. Was it *much* worse than this?" begged the little girl.

Aunt Molly put aside her Bible, moved her chair away from the light and closer to the stove. Propping her feet on the hearth at the front of the old-fashioned stove and folding her hands in her lap, she seemed to be preparing for a long story. The young people forgot their game and magazines and listened with Kit to a story of more than sixty years ago.

Aunt Molly vividly told the story of her early home life and how members of her family were led to Christ through varied circumstances.

The silence that followed Aunt Molly's story was broken by Kit, who had an instictive aversion to silences.

"I think that's the best story I ever heard!"

Virginia soon insisted that Kit go to bed, for the hands of the clock were pointing to ten. Aunt Molly folded her quilt pieces, closed the Bible and let Steve help her upstairs. As Sherry watched them go, she turned to Virginia with a sigh of exasperation.

"Isn't she the dearest bit of nonsensical gullibility you ever met? Almost she could make me believe that tale. She should have been a novelist."

Virginia did not answer. What would have been the use of battling such deliberate perversity as Sherry's?

Chapter Twelve

Steve pushed his chair back from the table and bowed to Virginia.

"Thank you for a bountiful meal—of toast and coffee—my lovely hostess. The snow has almost ceased to fall, and if I had some snowshoes I'd go out and bring back some fresh meat —if I could find a bear or a fine young deer."

"I'll take you up on that," cried Sherry, who was in high spirits this morning. "I'll provide the snowshoes, or skis, and I dare you to go hunting."

"What do you mean?"

"Come down cellar and I'll show you."

Steve lit the lantern that hung in the stairway, and together they descended into the cellar below, from which soon issued crashing and hammering mixed with laughter and an occasional cry of pain. Sherry made two trips up to the lumber room off the kitchen, but she would not let Kit see what it was that she carried back under her sweater.

It was almost an hour before they came up to display triumphantly two pairs of homemade skis. They were constructed from barrel staves, and although they were not handsome, they were substantial. It took another half-hour to clear enough snow from the back door to permit the hardy couple to crawl out, then more time to fasten the skis. But at last Steve and Sherry were ready to start, and after a preliminary turn around the machine shed, they headed across the pasture. Kit climbed onto the kitchen table and peered out above the drifts, watching the pair as they made their way clumsily along the fence.

"I'm glad Sherry wore her red jacket. I can see it better than Steve's gray one. Do you think they'll *really* go hunting?"

"They have no gun. They'll probably have a snowball fight, and perhaps a race on their new skis, and then come back."

"Well, they aren't racing now. They're just standing by the fence talking and resting, I guess. They look like they're mad. Steve put his hands on Sherry's shoulder and shook her. She jerked away and walked on. Now Steve's going after her. Why does he get so mad at her? I think she's one of my nicest people."

"I don't know. Don't let it worry you, Kitkin. Let them settle their difficulties alone. Are they coming back?"

"No, they're going on. I can't see very well because the snow is getting thick again. Oh, I want to go out, too. I *do*, Ginny!"

"I know it, Dolly. But it can't be done. Just be patient, and next year you'll be using a pair of skis of your own. I'll buy them for you."

"Honest? Oh, I'll try. Did you hear her, Aunt Molly? That's really and truly a promise, Ginny. I *am* getting better. I've been using a cane for a week now. And I haven't cried for two days. If you'd let me try, I could walk without even the cane."

"But you mustn't, dear. When Jim called up last night to see if we were buried under a snowdrift, he said that he is going to bring Dr. Sawyer with him the next time he comes down, and he'll give you a thorough examination. I think he'll tell you to throw the cane away. If he says we may, we'll have a celebration and pitch it 'over the fence and out'! But let's not cheat, Kit."

"O. K. I'll be good. But I *could* walk easy as easy." Kit turned to the window again. "They're gone! I can't see a thing. Maybe they're really hunting. What could they hunt, Aunt Molly? What things for hunting are there in these woods?"

"Not a thing in this deep snow. They'll be back 'fore long willin' to eat baked potatoes and cornbread and be thankful."

But they did not come soon, and Kit became weary of watching over the drift that banked the window. Her restlessness returned and she wandered from the kitchen where Virginia was washing dishes to the parlor where Aunt Molly was making up Steve's bed on the davenport.

"I like this room. If I had two good legs, I could play that funny organ. I'd like to stay in here."

"You'd better get back by the fire. When Steve comes back, maybe Virginny will let him build a fire in here. Then it will be all right for you to come in. Your grampaw loved that organ. He give it to your grammaw once on their weddin' anniversary. Come on out now. Let's work on the quilt."

But quilts did not interest Kit, and she went back to the window to watch. The snow was falling fast again, and she could not see past the machine shed. She turned disconsolately and started for her scrapbooks, but a noise at the back door made her hasten in that direction. The hunters were back, and the day's catch had been rewarding. Throwing the snow high on either side, Steve was shoveling a way through the drift by the door. Sherry was untying the ropes that bound a huge bundle to a hand sled. They loosened their skies and came tramping in with arms full.

"Who says we can't hunt? What do you call this, Aunt Molly?"

"I call it a ham, and it come out of my smokehouse. An, that's my sled? How did you get over *there*?"

"On our skis, and wasn't it fun!" exclaimed Sherry, setting a tin bucket on the table. "I hope none of these eggs are broken. I almost fell once. Steve robbed your hen's nests. He's a good robber."

While Virginia and Kit stood about and exclaimed, they

unloaded eggs, cabbages, turnips (at which Kit turned up her nose), several loaves of bread and a big can of cookies.

"For a lady that lives alone, you keep a well-stocked pantry, Aunt Molly," said Steve putting down a great can of milk. "I was sorry we couldn't bring more. But I was afraid the jars of fruit wouldn't ride so well. The milk and eggs were enough of a problem."

"I never like to get caught short of food," answered the old lady apologetically. "Nate's and Rosy's grand-younguns might come unexpected, an' that Steve Barrett is always raidin' my pantry."

"Oh! So that's why you knew your way around so well! You'd been there before."

"It has been my favorite eating place for nearly thirty years. I cut my teeth on the edge of Aunt Molly's pantry shelves."

Virginia looked in embarrassed amazement at the supplies that covered the kitchen table. She felt that she must offer to pay for at least a part of them, but did not want to offend her guests. She had a suspicion that Aunt Molly would be reimbursed from Steve's pocket. But Aunt Molly apparently did not consider payment, for she spoke in a tone of gratitude to the two who were now taking off their wraps.

"I'm mighty obliged to you for gettin' these. If I've got to stay here for two or three days, I want to do my share. Did Ed milk yet this mornin'?"

"Yes, and he was watering the animals when we got there."

"He's a good neighbor. Is he snowed in, too?"

"It's not quite as bad there as here. The hill protected him a bit. But you can't go back for awhile, Aunt Molly. A limb from the box elder fell across your kitchen roof. The chimney is down and one corner of the roof is caved in. You can't live in it until it can be fixed."

"But I'll *have* to get home!" she cried in distress. "The

weather will get in, an' there's things in the pantry that'll freeze. I can ride them barrel staves as well as Sherry can!"

"Oh, no, you don't. You'd never make it. Sherry is built for drifts and you aren't. Anyway, we fixed things up. We carried everything to the cellar that might freeze, and moved things away from that corner. Ed and I put a tarpaulin over the roof and tied and weighted it down and it'll be all right. I'll go down tomorrow and get more stuff, and as soon as a team can get through, Ed will come up and get you and you can see for yourself."

The snow continued to fall. In the afternoon Steve tried to go into the village, but gave it up before he reached the highway. The radio, which was a valued connection with the great world outside, told of stalled trains, closed schools, disrupted communications. It was the heaviest snowfall in the history of the state, and the cold weather gave no promise of a thaw. Steve fretted at being away from his office and longed for his mail, but the drifts piled higher and all business was at a standstill in the little community.

"I could make it into town," confided Steve to Sherry, "but I couldn't come back every evening. There aren't enough hours in the day to permit a round trip. And I'm not leaving you women here alone."

"Go ahead! I can carry out ashes and shovel coal as well as you can, and Virginia's no slouch. We'll get along fine."

"Nothing doing. You're tough as an Indian, but Virginia isn't used to this, and—"

"And you'd rather stay here, anyway. For a seasoned old bachelor who loves to tell other folks how to run their lives, your sentiments do you credit. You're developing some regular adolescent complexes. Couldn't be in love by any chance, could you?"

Steve's face turned red and he busied himself with the fire as Virginia came into the room.

"Doesn't this room smell *nice?*" said Kit settling herself in the platform rocker. "And isn't this a classy chair? Fringe on the arms, and the loveliest squeak!"

"It looks like a museum piece," said Virginia. "But I like it. It reminds me of Grandpa. He used to sit here on Sunday afternoons and read the Bible—that great big one on the table—and rock and rock. The chair squeaked then, too."

"Wow! What a lapful the Book must have made!"

Between the Old and New Testaments were several pages for the family record, and Virginia read aloud the things about her grandfather's life that she had never known—his birth more than one hundred years ago, his marriage to Lyda Ann Sutton, the births of five children.

"I didn't know that!" she said with a break in her voice. "I thought my grandfather was his only child."

"He was the only one that growed up," said Aunt Molly. "I guess that's why he set so much store by him."

"Grandpa used this Bible for a file of his treasures," Virginia said tenderly, with a catch in her voice. These things were bringing back with them pictures of the old man who had been a very important part of her childhood and who had been almost forgotten in the busy years since he left them.

Steve had picked up a page of coarse paper—the kind used in school for scratch paper—and was intently trying to decipher the uneven writing that covered it. After some minutes of this perusal he burst out excitedly.

"Listen here, folks, this may be a real find! Aunt Molly, did Allie May have a nickname—one that old Joe Martin called her?"

"I can't recall. It sorto' seems so—I can't jes' remember."

"Oh, I do!" cried Virginia with a laugh. "He called her 'Banty' because he said she acted like a banty rooster. She was so little and so scrappy. Why do you ask?"

"Here's why! Listen."

He read from the paper slowly. The pencil marks were dull and the paper was ragged as if from much handling.

Dear Grampa. We are going away. Grampa Neil says we haf to. He won't live by you cause you think

he didn't give Daddy that money. I have cried and
cried and I prayed but I gess God doesn't like me cause
Mother and I hunted everplace and we can't find
the money. I don't think anything is nice any more.
I wish we was all dead. I was going to put this in
Jim's and my post office but you might not find
it so I'll sneek it into your mailbox. They won't tell
me where we are going but it's where you won't see me
nomore. I love you Grampa even if you make me
awful sorry. Banty.   P.S. I think the place we are
going is named Ke---ow.

"That name is right on a fold and part of it is gone," said
Steve as he finished reading. "But it ought to help a bit."

For a few minutes they sat in silence. The picture of a
heartbroken little girl smuggling this letter to the old man
who had been her closest companion for ten years, and who
had suddenly been harshly separated from her by suspicion
and hate, was so touching that they found no words to
speak of it.

Chapter Thirteen

The next morning was clear and bright. The sun shone on the white drifts piled against the fences and along the roads. Steve dug away the snow from the windows and doors so that the light could come in, unhindered, again.

"I feel all bleached out like a worm that just crawled out from a deep, deep cellar," said Sherry, reveling in the brightness of the dining room.

Aunt Molly could not get across the field to her little house, but Ed Harnish had telephoned that all was well, so she settled down as a part of the Martin household. Steve repaired his barrel-stave skis and after he had fixed the fires, filled all the coal buckets, carried in water and brought milk and eggs for the day, he again started for the village. Kit and Virginia stood at the window watching him until he passed out of sight over the hill, then turned back to the house which seemed strangely empty with no man to take charge.

In the late afternoon Steve returned. He was wearing real snowshoes and was dragging a toboggan which was piled high with bundles—groceries, fresh meat, fruit and, best of all, the mail which had accumulated for several days. A big brown envelope from Jim contained several letters from Mother. As yet she did not know of the girls' residence at the farm, so all mail was sent via Jim. While Kit feasted on a fat letter addressed to her, Virginia read the others. Mother approved the plan to take Dad to New York, but could not say when it would be possible.

I am learning new lessons of trust every day. It is just a case of a step at a time with my hand in the Lord's. Your letters are a wonderful tonic for me. I wish Dad could share them. He lies here so quietly and so unreachable that it makes me feel inexpressibly alone. But I turn to the One who is always near and He gives strength as I need it. I thank Him daily for the four dear children who are helping me by their prayers. God bless you all. Perhaps sooner than we think we will be together again.

Lovingly,
MOTHER

Mother's letters always brought tears of homesickness to Kit, and now even Virginia wiped her eyes and bit her lip at the thought of Dad's lying still and unknowing while Mother sat by his side in that faraway strange land.

Jim's letter was short. He was well but busy. He had been assured by telephone that they were well provided for in the emergency caused by the blizzard, so would not try to get down before Christmas. Perhaps by then the word from Mexico would be more definite.

When I come I hope to have another piece of news for you. Life has been tough this fall but it has had compensations. Hope you'll all like the news I bring. Until then, my love to both of you. You're a swell pair of sisters and two good sports.

As ever,
JIM

A note from Kurt inquired about the holidays:

If you have a warm room where I can have several hours of quiet each day, I'd like to work on a hard term paper. I can't do so well here as there's always too much noise. I need the inspiration of Kit's pestiferousness, anyway. And I'm dying to see the old house. I can't remember it though I was a mature three-year-old when last I saw it. So let me know. If you can accommodate me, I'll be there with bells on.

KURT

Kit fairly quivered with excitement as she heard these letters. She balanced on the good leg and held her cane high in the air.

"Oh, oh, if Daddy would only wake up and if Kurt and Jim would come for Christmas, I'd be so happy. Do you think I can go without even a cane then, Ginny? I use it such a little now."

"Wait and see, honey. Let's let the doctor decide."

"I'm sure it'll be all right. I can't wait!"

Kit's voice was shrill with excitement. Her tears were forgotten as she began to plan enthusiastically.

"We'll have to have fires in every room then, and we'll all sing carols by this nice old organ, and—"

"If we have to have so many fires, Mr. Kurt Martin will find out what a coal bucket is," said Virginia grimly. "He'll discover, as I have, why furnaces were invented."

"There's another stove in the lumber room. Kurt and I can move it up to the north bedroom and it will make a study for an incipient Kappa. Once when I was a small boy I stayed here two weeks while my dad was away and Aunt Molly had a houseful of other guests, and I was warm as toast," said Steve.

"I'm going to have a load of coal brought out when the road is opened," said Sherry. "I haven't paid enough for my shelter and heat, and I want to get in on it before I get set out in the cold."

"You'd better charge me room rent, too," put in Steve. "I'd like to stay tonight, if you don't mind. Tomorrow I'll go back to my own quarters, but I'd hate to tackle that trek back tonight. I'm far from being a ski champion."

"Of course you can stay," answered Virginia. "I don't know what we would have done without you."

All day Sherry had proved herself a pleasant and helpful part of the household. She had helped with the cooking and dishwashing, designed a new quilt-block pattern for Aunt Molly, led Kit in a victorious battle with fractions, had meekly taken a lesson in accounting from Steve and, as a climax to the day, had bundled Kit up and taken her for a ride on the sled.

"We went down to the bridge by the tree where you and

Jim and Allie May used to play. Sherry said that if I wasn't lame she'd upset me in a drift. I'm coming back here next year and walk on snowshoes like Sherry."

All in all it was a happy day, and Virginia hoped it would end on a pleasanter note than the previous ones had. Aunt Molly, too, felt relieved at the change in the atmosphere and looked forward to a quiet evening as the young people browsed through old books and magazines or played games.

But hardly had Kit left them before the argument began, with Sherry as the aggressor. Aunt Molly did not participate, for it was beyond her depth, so she sat quietly, sewing and praying and troubled at what she heard even though she could not understand it, for through the unintelligible argument she sensed Sherry's doubt and bewilderment.

Such phrases as "the ultimate truth," "man's postulates," "naturalistic philosophy" and "machinist or purposivist" had no meaning at all for her. But when Sherry defined Christianity as "an escape mechanism" and prayer as a "reflex influence," Aunt Molly was troubled and sick at heart. To Aunt Molly, Christianity was not a mechanism, not a philosophy. It was a Person, the One Altogether lovely, the Saviour of her soul, the Lord of her life. And prayer was a simple turning to her Father for the filling of every need in her life and the expression of her gratitude to Him.

Not being able to contribute anything to the debate, she folded her work and climbed the stairs to her room. Here, while the three young people argued until midnight, the old woman, who did not know the meaning of all the theories and speculations but who knew the Saviour intimately through long years of walking in daily companionship with Him, knelt by her bed and prayed for them all. She prayed for Sherry first of all, that the Holy Spirit might show her her need and lead her to the One who could resolve all her doubts and free her from her fears. For Steve she asked that the faith which had, until recently, been only an intellectual possession might become a more vital part of him, stirring his heart and opening his eyes to new channels of life and service. She prayed that Virginia might learn to trust self less and God more, that she might recognize her own insufficiency and trust His sufficiency. She pleaded that Kit might be kept pure and trusting and ere long be well and strong again. Then one more prayer went up—a prayer for the little girl who thought God no longer cared for her.

"Wherever she is tonight, Father, speak to her heart and reveal Thy love to her. And bring her back to us. Amen."

After the house was quiet and Sherry's even breathing from the cot in the corner told that she was asleep, Virginia lay wide awake.

I can't imagine what could make her so desperately sad, she mused. *Steve says her folks all love her and she hasn't lost anyone dear to her, by death. Perhaps some so-called Christian proved unworthy. Maybe she loved some man and found out he wasn't true. But that wouldn't make her angry at her parents and brother. Well, whatever the trouble is, it could be overcome if she only knew God. If I could just show her—*

She felt very much ashamed of herself as she realized that in all the twelve years since she had become a Christian she had never thought of her duty as a witness for Him. Now, with the spiritual need of Sherry Carlson crying out to her, she was eager to begin her task.

She would not talk or argue with Sherry. She would, instead, show her the joys and perfections of the obedient Christian life. She would be lovable, kind, gracious and thoughtful. She would not be annoyed at Sherry's perversity and would be patient with Kit's petulance. She would do so well the work that was hers to do that Sherry would have to acknowedge that Christianity had to be true. With a sight of relief at having reached this satisfactory conclusion, Virginia fell asleep.

Chapter Fourteen

For a few days the campaign of demonstration went along smoothly. The roads were open again, mail was coming regularly, and Virginia was able to get out to church and into the village for supplies. Steve was occupied with an intensive search for Allie May and they seldom saw him. There was little to annoy Sherry, and as Kit was feeling unusually well there was no friction. Virginia felt that a few obstacles would be welcome as an opportunity to show her new understanding of her task in life. Perhaps Sherry felt that something was needed to liven them, for one afternoon when Aunt Molly and Kit were asleep she tried to start again the argument about the Bible. But Virginia would not rise to the bait even when Sherry accused her of being afraid to argue without Steve's assistance. Then Sherry endeavored to "stir up a more invigorating atmosphere," as she said, by attacking Virginia's favorite theories of teaching. But Virginia listened in silence and when Sherry had finished propounding her absurd doctrines, said, with a laugh, "I hope you get a chance to try out your theories some time. It would be very interesting to note the results."

Sherry gave up the effort then but, as if she sensed what Virginia was trying to do, she began a campaign of her own to tease and irritate as much as possible. She shirked her share of the work, teased Kit until she reduced her to tears, ceased to help Aunt Molly with her sewing, spent hours grumbling at any real or imaginary grievance she could find, and made herself so generally disagreeable that Steve tried to get Virginia to ask her to leave.

"I could get Mrs. Tucker in the village to take her for awhile. Her niece that has been with her has gone. I'm going up to Uncle's again soon and I will try to work at that end of the tangle again."

"I don't want her to leave. I don't mind her at all. I am trying to show her that a Christian can keep sweet and true under fire, and I think she has caught on and is trying to break me. Let us alone, Steve, and see if I can't make a demonstration that will win her approval."

After two weeks of this, however, Sherry lost interest in such an unavailing project. Christmas was coming and there was so much of pleasant activity about that she was drawn back into the midst of it before she was quite aware of what was happening. Kurt arrived, laden with typewriter, books, skis and skates. He found in Sherry a playmate who could keep up with him on the longest hike and who did not fear the steepest hill. Kurt's coming was as if a door had opened and let a fresh, invigorating breeze into a stuffy, closed room. The small bickerings were forgotten.

When Jim drove down the day before Christmas he brought Dr. Sawyer with him. Kit was taken to the office of Dr. Hardy in the village, and for an hour she underwent an examination that overlooked no possibility of hidden trouble. After it was over the doctors looked at each other, then at Kit, then at Jim and Virginia, and back to Kit.

"Do you want a nice present for tomorrow, Kit?"

"Oh, yes!"

"If you'll be careful—real careful—and not go skiing or cut any fancy figures on the ice, you can put your cane in the closet and forget about it."

"Really?"

"Yes, really. Mind, though, I said you'd have to be careful. But you've done so much better than I thought you could that I almost think that by summer you can be back on those skates again."

It was hard to think of this holiday as a merry Christmas with the knowledge of Dad's condition hanging over them. But they tried. Steve was invited to dinner and insisted on furnishing the biggest turkey he could buy. Aunt Molly's house was not yet repaired, for the carpenter's examination revealed rotten beams that would have to be replaced and this work would require additional time and more favorable weather, so she was still with them, and they secretly hoped she would have to stay as long as they did. But Sherry was not at the Christmas feast. She had gone to bed the day before with a sore throat and her dinner had to be carried on a tray to the room where she lay surrounded with a pile of the old magazines of which she was so fond.

"You just go ahead and have a good time and forget about me," she said when Kit stood in the door and lamented her illness.

"But I wanted you to see Jim!"

"Yes, I know you did. But Jim will probably be just as happy *not* to meet me. He'll never know what he missed."

So Kit went back downstairs frowning about her disappointment. But with Kurt playing Christmas carols on his mouth organ and with Jim giving her bits of news from her friends in the home neighborhood, she could not stay sad. Then, at the dinner table Jim upset all her plans and announced his engagement to Dot Blackwell. Kurt and Virginia exclaimed in pleasure as Kit, herself, would have done a few months ago. But now she could only stare in sick amazement until Jim saw her and asked, "What's the matter, Puss? I thought you liked Dot."

"Oh, Dot's all right. But I wanted you to marry Sherry!"

"Well, that's too bad. But you see, I love Dot and I've never even seen Sherry."

"That's the trouble. If you'd seen her you couldn't help but love *her*."

"Oh, couldn't he?" groaned Steve. "Then for his sake I'm glad she had tonsilitis."

"I'll tell you what, Kitten," said Kurt, "I'll marry Sherry

if she'll wait until I'm through college and have made my fortune."

Kit considered this, and said reluctantly, "I guess that'll have to do. But I never thought of you as anybody's husband."

"Give me time, kid. Give me time."

So Kit's dream of getting Sherry into the family had to be stored away until such time as she could dust it off and use it on Kurt.

When Virginia came into the parlor after the dishwashing was finished, Steve and Jim were discussing the search for Allie May.

"I thought I had my hands almost on her a few days ago. I wrote to all the colleges and universities in these five states, and they sent the names of many Martins who had graduated in the last ten years or were still enrolled. Among them was one Alice M. Martin. I hied me to the little backwater college that had sent me the name, and dug out her present address and name. I had all sorts of anticipatory thrills as I drove to see her. I remembered Virginia's description—'small, dark and petite', and I felt I would recognize her immediately. Well, I found her. She was large, blond and blue-eyed and had never been in this state. So— exit Allie May. I'm back at the beginning."

"Did you ever figure out the name of the town you wrote me about—the one she mentioned in her note to Gramps?" asked Jim.

"No. I've looked up every place resembling it, and none of them click."

"Let's look at it again," said Kurt eagerly. "No little old berg can get away from me."

They studied the penciled scrawl once more. The word had been written just where the paper was folded and had worn away until part of it was completely gone.

"K- - -ow," read Kurt." That ought not to be so hard. Can't we get a gazetteer and look up all the names that begin with *K* and end with *ow*? Or maybe she couldn't spell any better than her cousin Jim. The name might begin with C. We could try."

"That we could," said Jim, overlooking the reference to his weakness. "Do you suppose there's any atlas here that would help us?"

"The only atlas here has been studied from cover to cover. While we were snowbound we made a game of it and went through it on an average of at least twice a day," answered Steve. "I don't know where to turn next. I've advertised in papers all over the country. I've looked up Martins in every state in the Union. Ormand isn't an ordinary name but I can find no trace of it."

"Have you looked in the buryin' ground?" asked Aunt Molly.

"Yes, I even did that. I thought that Neil or his wife might have passed away by this time and been buried over at Sparta. Neil's parents were buried there and many people like to return their dead to lie among old home scenes. But I couldn't learn a thing. There were only three graves on the Orland lot, those of Neil's parents and an unnamed infant brother. There were three graves that had no markers on an adjoining lot, and the sexton thought they were Ormands but all the records were burned three years ago when the office caught on fire, so he couldn't be sure. I think the lot must have been sold to someone else. I wanted to hunt up some old resident to see if he might remember, but Sherry was with me that day and she insisted she had to get home. She called me a ghoul, and made such scornful remarks about grave robbers that I rather lost my zeal for that part of the search."

"Yes," said Virginia, "she came home in a fury. She said she thought us all cruel to force ourselves on a poor girl who asked nothing but to be left alone."

"That's one side of it," said Jim in his deliberate way. "If I thought Allie May knew we were hunting her and really didn't want to be found, I'd quit the search right now. But she may be homesick and lonesome and needing us.

Or she may need money. Aunt Alice may be dead, too, and Banty would be all alone, in that case. Neil Ormand had plenty of money to leave her, but it may have been lost in some wild speculation. Until we know that Allie May doesn't need us we must keep on hunting."

"That's the way I feel." Virginia sighed. "And I was so hopeful that we could find her for Daddy before he comes back."

"We'll keep on trying," Steve assured her. "If any of you has any bright ideas I'll gladly receive them."

But no one could offer suggestions, and the talk drifted to the matter of bringing Dad back to the States.

"Mr. Hudson talked to the mission doctor when he was in Texas last week. A telephone call isn't too satisfactory but it's better than a letter. The doc thinks Dad can be taken down the mountain in about six weeks. Said the road had been washed out by heavy rains and they'd have to wait until it was fixed. Dr. Sawyer has made the arrangements with the hospital and surgeon in New York, so when I get the word I'll go on to meet Mother."

Jim's voice was brisk and cheerful, and Kit gave Kurt's hand a squeeze. Mother and Daddy were coming home! The world would be all right again. But Virginia, looking into Jim's eyes, read the doubt and concern there and felt a sick fear clutch her heart.

In the late afternoon Jim started back to the city, promising to let them know at once if he received news. Hardly had he gone when Sherry appeared downstairs, "clothed and in her usual mind" as Steve expressed it. When Aunt Molly voiced concern, she laughed and said, "I am afraid I'm going to recover. In fact, I don't think I ever was sick. I just thought I might be!"

She sat down at the old organ and began to play. Soon they were laughing at her imitations of well-known singers. After all, one might as well laugh at Sherry. She couldn't be understood, so why try?

"There! That's better," she said whirling around on the

stool. "What a bunch of sourpusses you were when I came in. You must have been discussing Allie May. Let's forget that black sheep for awhile and do something stimulating. I know a new way to play charades. Kit and Kurt and I will play Steve and Ginny and lick them black and blue."

She soon explained her game and had them playing with zest. All thought of Allie May was banished and the day had a happy ending in spite of the shadows that lurked around the corner.

Chapter Fifteen

It was three days later that the letter came from Allie May. Sherry had met Steve as he left the post office, and when he told her about it she insisted that he go out to the farm at once to let Virginia know. After the years of fruitless searching it was almost unbelievable that at last they had a letter from her. But the missive itself was small comfort.

> Dear Mr. Barrett:
>
> I have seen your advertisement in several papers. Won't you please quit hunting and forget about me? I don't think you will ever find me. I will do all I can to prevent it. I have put all that life behind me and am trying to forget it.
>
> If the money should ever be found, I would like to come back. It would be nice to see Jim and Ginny again. But Grandpa and Grandpa Neil said things to each other that I can never forget. As long as folks think that my daddy or Grandpa Neil stole that money I don't want to belong to the Martin family. Mother and both of my grandparents are gone. I am alone and am sufficient for myself.
>
> I know how hard you are hunting for me. I know lots of things that would startle you if I told them. I have been so close to you at times that I could touch you. You did not know me then, and I don't think you ever will. Let's call it quits. Take the farm and all that's in the house. I have plenty of money of my own.
>
> ALLIE MAY
>
> P.S. Tell Ginny I meant to wash my cereal bowl that night but she almost caught me.
> P.P.S. I kissed you once, Mr. Barrett. Don't you remember?

They looked at each other in amazement. Kurt was the first to speak. "What does she mean about a cereal dish?"

Virginia told them of that first night in the farmhouse, and of the signs she discovered which indicated another occupant.

"I even saw her! In the dim light I thought it was my own reflection in the hall mirror. When I realized that the supposed reflection had on a white blouse while my dress was dark, I almost died of fright. And when I went to the kitchen at two in the morning and found a hot lamp chimney I thought I couldn't stay here. I locked Kit and myself in our bedroom and lay frozen with fear the rest of the night. The next morning I found a cereal dish in the sink, and some of the milk in the bottle had been used. Do you wonder that I received Sherry with open arms when Steve brought her here?"

"You're a swell sport to go through that and not run out on the game," said Kurt approvingly. "And to think that Allie May has been here, right in the house!"

"She's some gal." Sherry chuckled. "And she kissed Steve! How gay!"

She sat on the floor with her arms clasped around her knees and rocked with laughter.

"Oh, Stevy, Stevy! Why didn't you tell us? A woman in your life! Where have you hidden her?"

"I haven't hidden her and I didn't kiss her!" he protested.

"She didn't say you did. She said that *she kissed you.*" said the literal Kit.

"I wish she weren't so stubborn," wailed Kit. "I want to see her worse than anything. Is is wrong for me to pray that we'll find her, Ginny."

"Of course not, dear. It's never wrong to pray for what we need."

"Then why don't we pray? Why don't we *all* pray?"

She looked about at the others but no one answered.

"Don't the rest of you like to pray, too? Why don't we

pray together? I get lonesome praying alone. Mother and
I pray together when she's home. I want us *all* to pray."

Steve looked at Virginia inquiringly. Her face flushed but
she looked gravely back at him. Aunt Molly's voice broke
the silence.

"That's the most sensible suggestion anybody's made yet.
If you children'll join with me, we'll just lay all this affair
in the lap of the Lord right now."

Kit began to pray with a jumble of childish words that
told how this desire had lain on her heart. Her plea was a
mixture of petitions that Allie May might be discovered and
that their parents might return soon. As they listened, both
Virginia and Kurt realized how the little girl's heart had
ached for her parents during the hard months past, and
each resolved to do more to help her. Kurt prayed in a few
short boyish sentences. Virginia had not heard him pray
since he was a small boy, and in that minute she felt closer
to her brother than she had been in years. She wondered
how Sherry felt about this. She tried to think how she
would word her own prayer. She wanted Sherry to feel the
full impact of such a witness. But when Steve's short prayer
was finished there was a silence and she knew they were
waiting for her. She began, but the smooth phrases she had
planned would not come, and she found herself stammering
a maze of disjointed sentences. She realized that she had
asked that her parents might be discovered and that Allie
May might be healed and returned home. In confusion she
closed her petition and waited with the rest while Aunt
Molly poured out her soul before the throne. There were no
smooth phrasings, no trite terms. She was just a child,
troubled and needy, baring her heart to the Father. As they
listened, all felt the presence of the Spirit who could bring
peace and quiet into their disturbed lives. Burdens rolled
away. Heartaches were soothed, strength and wisdom for
their needs were assured.

When they rose from their knees, Virginia noticed that
Sherry was not in the room. She had not expected her to

pray, but she had hoped that she would kneel with them, and she felt a sense of disappointment that she had not done so.

As Kurt helped Kit to rise he gathered her close for a minute and whispered something that brought a quick smile to her face. Virginia wanted to fold them in her arms and hold them securely against the buffetings that life was sure to bring.

"I must be getting back to town," said Steve. "I left a lot of work undone when I found that letter in my box. Don't you want to walk out to my car with me, Virginia? It's at the gate. That thaw today made the lane too slippery for traffic. Come on. You need fresh air."

As they made their way along the gravel path by the driveway, Steve spoke once more of his perplexing problem with Sherry.

"I feel like a cur to refuse to tell the folks where she is. I had a desperate letter from Don yesterday. Aunt is ill and he thinks it's grief that caused it. That letter Sherry burned up was an apology from her mother and a plea from Don for her to come back and talk with them. When Aunt heard that Sherry wouldn't read it, she became ill. They think I'm at fault because I've kept her confidence. But I don't dare betray her presence here. They'd come and try to take her back and she'd do something desperate. Yet I feel like a heel to let you be saddled with her for so long. She's nobody's ray of sunshine."

"We like to have her—really we do. Please don't worry about that one minute. But I wish I could help her. If she would confide in us, Aunt Molly or I might help. But you can't work to any advantage in utter darkness."

"I wish I could help, but I know so little myself that I can tell you almost nothing. The whole affair probably started over some insignificant difference of opinion. You know how stubborn Sherry is, and Aunt is more than a little inclined to be dogmatic. Sherry may have aired some of her ideas on Christianity after she came home from college. I can't guess about the beginning of it. But it has grown in Sherry's mind until its size fills all her being. I don't believe she ever really thinks of anything else. She's consumed with anger against Don at present. Says he hasn't a vestige of backbone and is entirely under Aunt's thumb. There's too much of truth in that for me to argue with her, but I think the whole bunch of them would do anything to get her back, and if she'd give them a chance they might prove to her that they'd learned a lesson. But until Sherry takes a different attitude I wouldn't dare tell where she is. That would upset the apple cart!"

"Just leave her alone for awhile. Maybe we're making more progress with her than we can see."

Steve took Virginia's arm to guide her around the puddles which the day's warmth had left in the path. As they went along, Virginia pondered on how close she felt to this friend whom she had known only a few months. In that time he had grown into their lives so firmly that he seemed a friend of many years. She thought of the prayer circle in the parlor and of her own inadequate petition. To no one else would she have spoken of it, but with Steve's hand on her arm and his eyes on her face she found herself speaking with a freedom that surprised her.

"I wanted *so* much to show Sherry how much God means to us. I'm trying to live so that she will believe that there is something worth while in my faith. But I always get bothered when I try to say anything. My prayer was awful. I guess it's a good thing she didn't hear it."

"You were all right. I don't do so well myself when praying aloud. I pray in Sunday school often, but I'm afraid that I have a sort of form that gets to be rather lifeless. When I hear someone like Aunt Molly pray I realize that I'm only a beginner in the school of prayer."

"That's the way I feel. But I'm glad I've begun. Maybe the things that have happened this last year are the things that will help to advance me in that school."

They had reached the road and Steve paused now with his hand on the car door.

"I try to realize how hard it must be for you. But it's a bit difficult for me to feel badly about it because it was through those same difficulties that I was allowed to meet you, so, to me, the silver lining sticks out all around the cloud."

As she went back to the house the early sunset was coloring the west and making the windows red with its reflection. The cheerful glow reminded her of the warmth and welcome within. Suddenly she knew that she loved this place. In spite of the sorrows and hardships she had known here, in spite of her parents' absence—perhaps *because* of these things—she was a bigger, stronger person than she had been six months before. This old house would always be remembered as the garden spot where her soul had made new growth.

"If I didn't want so badly to get back to teaching, and if there were just a *few* of the comforts of life here, I would like to stay. Maybe I could teach here. I probably won't have much of a job left at home. There's something so *solid* in a place like this. I feel more a part of it than I ever did of the big house in town.

"I hope we don't have to sell it. Yet it's foolish to keep it with no farmers in the family. I wish I were a man. I'd farm. Or I wish Allie May would turn up and want to keep the place. It seems to belong to her more than to us. But she said she wouldn't come back unless we found the money. If we could do that, we could put an ad in the paper and tell her so. Oh, I hope we can. It's at least worth trying."

Chapter Sixteen

Virginia broached her plan to Sherry at the earliest opportunity. That unpredictable young lady was immediately interested.

"I never have thought much of your efforts to dig Allie May out of hiding, but her letter shows that she'd like to come back if the money was found. So let's find it!"

"While we are shut in the house we can search it room by room. Uncle Fred *might* have come into the house and put the money away somewhere and then gone out again. I don't think they thought of that. It seems to me that they only spoke of hunting outside. We'll go over every inch of the house. Then when it's warmer we'll go over the barn and machine shed and even the chicken coops. We've *got* to find that money!"

Sherry's enthusiasm dimmed suddenly. "But if Neil Ormand never paid him that money, you won't find it."

"But he did pay him. I'm sure of that. And I'm just as sure that Uncle Fred put it where he meant Grandpa to find it. He probably got sick on the way home and put the money away and then started out to tell Grandpa he was ill. Come on! Let's get busy."

Aunt Molly and Kurt and Kit were told of the scheme and all other projects were laid aside for this major undertaking. Even Kurt's term paper was forgotten.

They decided to search the parlor first. Every book was taken out of the bookcase and Aunt Molly patiently leafed through each. The drawers of the desk were opened and each

paper unfolded and every box opened. This proved an in-
terresting task, and time and again they forgot the object
of their search in their interest in these varied papers and
articles which told of the life of the man whose personality
still seemed to permeate the place. Notebooks filled with
figures giving weights of loads of grain, measurements of
corncribs, prices of stock or crops. Rusty pens, stubs of
pencils, a few old coins, a great claw from some animal,
queer stones, an unusual knot formation from a tree, a
polished buckeye, a pearl-handled knife.

"I used to long to go through these drawers," said Virginia.
"I imagined that they held the most interesting things on
earth."

"Well, they don't seem to hold any trace of five hundred
dollars," said Sherry tapping the back of the case to be sure
that it held no secret panels.

They took the pictures from the wall and removed them
from their frames, even though they admitted that Fred
Martin certainly had not hid the money in such an unlikely
place.

"The only way to hunt for things is to look *everyplace*,
even the places you know are impossible," said Kurt, pulling
the small nails from a frame with his pocketknife. "This paper
back of the picture here is dated about thirty years ago and
—what's this?"

They crowded around while he unfolded a piece of paper
and read, "Right to 18, left to 26, right to 5, left to 31."

"Sounds like the combination to a safe. Do you think there
might be a safe hidden somewhere?"

"I don't think so," said Aunt Molly. "If they was, Joe
Martin would of knowed it. One thing I'm sure of. He looked
everywhere he knowed."

They tapped the bricks around the chimney, and took the
tacks out of the carpet and looked under the edges.

"This seems pretty silly," said Virginia as she struggled
with the rusty tacks." Uncle Fred surely didn't have time

to take up the carpet! But we said we'd look every place, so here goes!"

It took two days to complete that one room, but when they had finished they were convinced that the money was not in the parlor. They searched the dining room next and did it in one afternoon, for there was only one cupboard with dish shelves above and linen drawers below. In a teacup on the top shelf they discovered a handful of discolored nickels and pennies, apparently some special fund. But no bills.

"Let's take the lumber room next," said Kurt. "If we build a fire in the laundry stove, it will be warm enough, and I've been itching to dig into that room. I've only got two more days. I have to be back on the campus Saturday."

"I've been wanting to root in that junk pile ever since I came," put in Sherry. "I wouldn't be surprised if we found something that was buried there during the Civil War—the family plate or jewels that were hidden to keep them from the invading army."

"Considering the fact that the invading army didn't get near this place by a thousand miles or so, you must think my ancestor was pretty scary."

"Not scary, Kurt. Just cautious. Anyway, we might find *something*."

"I'll settle for five hundred dollars," said Virginia, as she began to prepare supper. "I'm not a whit interested in Civil War relics. I just want to find that money and convince Allie May that we want her. If she knew how hard we were working to be able to convince her, I'm sure she'd come home. Well, we'll start on the lumber room tomorrow and we'll have to work like beavers to finish in two days."

"I know one thing that would help," said Kurt returning from the lumber room where he had been looking over the next day's work. "It looks to me as if there are magazines from fifty years back piled in the corners. If we ever settle this estate we can pay court costs by calling in the junk man and selling the lot to him. I'd suggest that we haul them all out into the dining room where you girls can go through them at your leisure. I don't think there's one chance in ten million that Uncle Fred would hide money in an old magazine. But we're not overlooking even that ten-millionth chance. So what say I leave the magazines for you?"

"I agree, and we could move them out tonight so that we can get an early start tomorrow. We'll need to make good use of your manly strength; some of those boxes look heavy. I have no idea what's in them but we will find out."

The next morning Kurt built a roaring fire in the laundry stove and lit the two lanterns that hung on the wall.

"These little windows are too small to let in enough light, so we'll have to depend on these old fellows to brighten the corners where we are."

There was no attic in the farmhouse, so all the things that usually collect in an attic were crowded into this room. There were boxes of outmoded clothing, discarded household equipment, barrels of empty fruit jars, cans of nails and screws, broken pieces of furniture, boxes of cotton, wool and silk scraps, an old trunk containing, among other things, a blue uniform which Aunt Molly said must have been the one that belonged to Joe Martin when, as a schoolboy, he ran away and joined the army in '63.

Aunt Molly was quick to recognize many an article, and would greet it as if it were an old friend.

"Well, that's that," Kurt said as the second afternoon waned. "I feel as if we've moved the Smithsonian Institute. I'm all for quitting. Here and now I bequeath any work yet to be done in this room to you ladies. I'm going back to college. I hope I can get my term paper finished when I get back to the dorm. The bedlam we have there is a dead calm compared with the so-called 'quiet' of this place."

After he had gone the girls worked doggedly at their self-imposed task. But room after room yielded no clue to the missing bills whose discovery might bring Allie May back to them.

Chapter Seventeen

The thrill of the hunt was gone and it had settled down into a routine that sometimes grew tedious. But they persisted, determined that no inch of the house should remain untouched when warmer weather would let them out of doors. The upstairs rooms with their closets filled with quilts and clothing, the bedroom where the girls slept, even the cellar, were all searched thoroughly but yielded no money. There was one result, however. In the course of the search the girls, united in a common interest, grew to know each other in a more intimate way than their former relationship, with Kit and Aunt Molly always about, had afforded. There developed between them a camaraderie that lightened their task and made the search a merry one in spite of their earnestness. Enjoying this fellowship, Virginia yearned anew to lead Sherry into the joy of a personal acceptance of Christ. She herself had learned many valuable lessons during these weeks, and knew that her spiritual life had been deepened and broadened. She had found that when her own strength was insufficient for the burden laid upon her she could go to the Source of all strength and draw upon Him for her needs. In the uncertainty that hung over them, with home disrupted, Dad ill and both parents far away, the certainties of the eternal truths had grown doubly precious. No wonder Sherry was so often sad! How could she be otherwise with no comfort for earth's sorrows, of which she appeared to have a full share, and no hope for the eternity hereafter. Oh, she *must* be convinced! It was unthinkable that she could not be shown her own need and Christ's sufficiency.

Baffled by Sherry's unresponsiveness, Virginia wrote to her pastor at the home church, asking him to send her books that might be more convincing than her own arguments. He answered promptly with a package so large that she wondered if she could ever read all the volumes. There were several books, heavy in size and content, by theologians whose names meant nothing to her but whose works must have commanded great respect among students of the subject, for Dr. Connor wrote that they were leaders in the field of Christian apologetics. There was a volume by a professor in a well known Bible School, and one by the president of the seminary from which Dr. Connor had graduated. There were various paper bound books and booklets, and many tracts. The more she looked through them the more Virginia was appalled at the prospect of assimilating even a small portion of them. But if she could help Sherry she was willing to try. So she heroically undertook the task and spent many hours studying and seeking for evidences that would be indisputable even to one of Sherry's keen wit. Steve found her at it one morning when he came out to see Aunt Molly about the repairs for her house.

"What a stack of learning for one lady to tackle!" Steve exclaimed, as he saw her studying earnestly. "Do you expect to get it all down in one meal, or is it your week's intellectual menu spread out before you?"

Virginia explained, keeping her voice low so that it could not be heard in the dining room where Sherry was reading.

"Could I help any? May I have a couple of the weightiest tomes to carry home to my lair? I could review them and get the arguments pro and con lined up. A bit of legal training ought to come in handy. You do the same with your big book and then we'll tackle Miss Sherry together. I'm as anxious to see her won over as you are."

But when they did approach her with their combined arguments she was not impressed.

"You don't have to sling all that knowledge at me," she grinned impishly. "I won't argue with you at all. The Christian faith isn't a thing to be argued about. It's either true or it isn't. If it's true, then I'm all wrong and I've sure missed the boat. If it isn't true, it's just an anesthetic that a lot of folks are using to dull the pain of living in this hateful world. I'd honestly like to believe it. Life would be easier. It's the most beautiful dream ever invented. But try as I will, I can't believe it."

"Do you prefer to believe, instead," asked Steve gravely, "that there isn't an eternity ahead of us for which we should be preparing? That we are all doomed to go out into oblivion without a ray of light in the darkness? Or that we lie down to eternal sleep?"

"Eternal sleep might not be so bad. Nothing could be worse than the things this life can do to a fellow. Oblivion would be better than an earth like this where nothing ever goes right, where folks who say they love you can hurt you terribly, and—oh, it would be better to be blotted out than to be the kind of person who ruins everything he touches!"

Virginia and Steve looked after her in dismay as she stalked from the room.

"We seem to make matters worse every time we try. I'll just have to keep on trying to show her by my life. But she doesn't want to be shown. I wonder sometimes why she doesn't get angry and leave us." Virginia sighed.

"She won't do that," Steve assured her. "She's as near to being happy here as she will ever be until she swallows her pride and goes back home. And I'm beginning to think she'll never do that."

"I keep thinking how badly her folks must feel. They want to find her as much as we want to find Allie May, don't they?"

"More so, if possible. I had another letter from Don today. I tried to read some of it to Sherry but she shrugged her shoulders and walked away. Well—that's that. I can't handle her. How goes the search for the elusive money?"

"We've been over the entire house from cellar to the farthest corner of the upstairs. No success. Kit's in the bedroom now looking through some boxes of old postcards and photographs. We went through them last week, but Kit can't give up. Finding Allie May before Dad comes home has become the big desire of her life. She doesn't know how slim the chances are for seeing Dad soon. She's always sure he will be back in a few weeks. I don't tell her of my own doubts on that subject. She thinks that if we could find the money, you could advertise again and tell Allie May about it."

"I could, but she'd probably think it was a trap. I think—"

"Ginny, oh, Ginny!" called Kit's excited voice from the bedroom. "Look what I found in this box of cards!"

They hurried in to find her excitedly holding up a small object.

"It's your little pearl ring, Ginny. You must have lost it when we were hunting. Did you know it was lost?"

"No, I didn't. And I can't imagine how it got there. I never wear it. It's so small I haven't been able to get it on for years. I must have dropped it out of my jewelry box when we cleaned the drawer that day last week. Remember we took everything out and looked behind the drawers."

She opened the box to replace the ring, then gave a startled cry. She looked closely at the ring, turning it over and over in her hand. At last she said in a voice that trembled, "This is not my ring. It is Allie May's."

"Allie May's" shrieked Kit, scrambling to her feet. "How did it get here?"

"Allie May's!" echoed Steve. "How do you know?"

"Because I have my own in my box, and this one has her initials in it. Grandpa gave them to us the last Christmas before Uncle Fred died. She must have lost it before they went away."

Later, when Kit was picking up the scattered cards and

they had returned to the living room, Virginia said to Steve, "I know that ring was not in that box last week. I took every one of those cards out and wiped out the box. I couldn't have missed it."

"Where did it come from, then?"

"Allie May has been back here again! *She's looking for the money, too.*"

"But when could she have had the chance?"

"I don't know. Maybe the night we all went to Sparta to the school concert. Or the night we drove to Harrisburg with you. Even Aunt Molly was away. Allie May *could* have slipped in then!"

"That would mean that she's living close enough to spy on you and know when you leave."

The thought was a disturbing one. But out of it came one bit of reassurance. It was voiced by Virginia as she walked to the road with Steve.

"It proves one thing. If she's still hunting that money, she wants to come back to us."

Chapter Eighteen

Virginia's resolution to give Sherry a demonstration of the Christian graces was often put to the test during those weeks when the weather kept them shut in from outside activities. Living in such a house in the days when modern conveniences were unknown did not call for any fortitude. One does not miss the things to which he has never been accustomed. But a girl who has been suddenly transplanted from a house equipped with all the labor-saving devices, that are an accepted part of today's living, to an old farmhouse boasting none will find life different and exceedingly difficult.

Every day they watched eagerly for the mailman's car. Until he had passed there was always a pleasureable anticipation in the air. There might be a letter. Often there was one from Jim or Kurt. Their friends from school and church kept them informed of all their activities, and Kit's schoolmates wrote frequently, but sometimes the news was not such as would lift the spirits. The letters from the high-school staff continued to mention the developing friendship of Howard Willis and Miss Terrant, and even though Virginia assured herself over and over that she no longer cared what Howard Willis did, the news made her wince.

It was hard, too, to wait week after week for the news from Mexico. It seemed years since they had all been together in the big house on Monterey Boulevard.

Not the least of Virginia's burdens was Kit. The doctor's permission for the cane to be abandoned had seemed to that young lady complete permission to resume her old activities. Virginia was sorely tried to restrain her as she daily became more daring and more insistent in her willfulness.

"I'm as good as new. I've really got two legs now. I don't hurt at all. I could slide down the hill, Ginny. I could, I know!"

"Not this year, Kitten. Dr. Sawyer said you'd be all well by summer. Let's be patient a little longer."

"But I'm not patient, ever, so how can I be patient a little longer? I want to slide down that hill so bad that I'm afraid that someday I just will!"

"Kit, don't you dare! I don't want to be cross, but you just *have* to mind."

"But I'm so tired of minding. I've minded and minded, and I feel like I just have to *not* mind, once!"

"You poor little chicken," said Virginia one day when she found Kit looking dolefully off toward the hill. "Ginny is as tired of this as you are, darling. But this is our job, and we have to stick to it. Maybe next year—"

"But we won't own the farm next year. I've prayed and prayed that we'd find Allie May before Dad comes. And when we do we'll sell the farm, so I have to slide this year!"

During these days of marking time there was one comforting source of help. Steve Barrett found many occasions to call. Sometimes he would spend the evening teaching Kit to play checkers. At other times he would be closeted alone with Sherry in an argument that left both of them in a state of depression. Or he would sit lazily watching Aunt Molly as she quilted or Virginia as she knitted busily on a sweater for Kurt. Often at such times he would look up and catch Sherry's eye and his face would flush as she winked teasingly at him.

Sometimes he would take Virginia for an evening of relaxation at Sparta, the county seat, and often when he had business in the country or a neighboring town he would take both her and Kit for a ride. Kit had admitted him to her heart on a level with Jim and Kurt, and he, in turn, gave her an affection that told more of his heart-hunger than he realized. To Virginia he was a bulwark against the fear and doubt that threatened her when days were dark. He did not question her, yet she often found herself telling him of her misgivings or of the disappointments of the day. He it was who gave her reassurance when her morale was low over the course of events at Claremont High. Although he did not know it, his friendship helped her over a bad spot when the home paper carried an announcement of the engagement of Howard Willis and Rae Terrant.

"I don't know what we would have done without you," she said one night as they were returning from Sparta. "Do all family lawyers give such self-forgetful service as you do?"

He laughed. "That's a question I can't answer. Being strictly honest, I have to admit that I don't know all the family lawyers in the world. The ones I have known, with the exception of my dad whose example I am trying to follow, were not too altruistic. Most of them were out to get what they could."

"The Martins are fortunate, then, in having fallen into the clutches of one of the less predatory members of the profession. When I think of how we've been cared for, not only by you but by Sherry and Aunt Molly, I am ashamed ever to doubt that God's hand is directing my steps."

"Lady dear, it's been a mutual affair. How do you think I could have managed Sherry without you? She would have been gone long ere this if it had not been for the Martins. And I would be hunting two girls instead of one. Sherry may have helped you with housework and expenses, but you have done more for her than even she realizes. As for Aunt Molly—well she could have stayed with Harnishes until her house was fixed, but they are crowded there and it would have been hard on all of them. As it is she has had the happiest winter she has known since her family has scattered."

"I've about given up finding Allie May. Ever since that letter came I've felt defeated. I know she wants to come back, but she won't do it without being able to clear her name. If she's living close enough to spy on us and know what we do, she's very clever. I don't think we'll find her until she wants us to, and that will never be!"

"I feel that I've failed your family completely. After my months of work I haven't a worth-while clue to give you. As a lawyer I'm a flop. As a friend I'm a fizzle!"

"Don't say such things. They aren't true! One discouraging case isn't a measure of your ability as a lawyer. And as a friend, you're super. Just count the friends who are dependent on you for help of some sort. There's Aunt Molly, whom you care for as if she were your mother. There's Sherry, who likes to tease you but who trusts you when she has turned against her parents. There are her folks, who take comfort in knowing that you are in touch with her. Then there are the Martins—all of us, from Dad to Allie May— whose affairs get a great deal more of your attention than can ever be paid for. We couldn't do without you!"

When he answered his voice showed that he had been touched by her outburst.

"Thanks. I'm not really so important, but it's nice to know that you think so. I've been a bit low lately over my girl troubles—Sherry and her tantrums and Allie May with her disappearing act. I talked to Don Carlson by phone last night. He says that if I don't tell them where Sherry is, the results will be disastrous for Aunt. And Sherry says Aunt is putting on an act, and that if I *do* tell, everyone will regret it. What to do I don't know."

They rode along in silence, pondering their mutual problems. Virginia knew that although he was discouraged, Steve would continue the search for Allie May, and her own discouragement of an hour before had changed to a hope that someday he would be successful. And Steve, in some inexplicable way, felt that he had shared his problem concerning Sherry and that it was on the way to solution.

Later, as they stood on the porch before parting, Steve said abruptly, "I'm just like most lawyers I guess—out to get what I can from my clients. I hope you know what I want from the Martin family!"

"Why, no—what—"

But he turned abruptly and left her with a hasty "Good night."

As she blew out the light that had been left burning for her and prepared for bed, she mused on Steve's words and was bewildered by possible interpretations that could be given them. Had Howard Willis made such a declaration, she would have known what he meant. But Steve Barrett was different!

Chapter Nineteen

Virginia had been half conscious several times during a night in late January that Kit's sleep was restless, but it was not until dawn that she finally aroused fully.

"What is it, Kitty? Are you ill?"

"I'm so hot. And my leg aches. I tried hard not to wake you, Ginny, but it really *hurts!*"

In alarm Virginia lit the lamp and examined the aching leg. There was no chance for doubt. There was a red area over the spot where the fracture had been, and Kit's temperature read 102 degrees. That could mean only one thing—a return of the infection they had believed was conquered. With heavy heart Virginia telephoned for the village doctor, and after a long-distance consultation with Dr. Sawyer, it was decided to take Kit back to the hospital in the city where Dr. Sawyer himself could treat her. Steve volunteered to take them so that they would not have to wait for Jim to come. Sherry insisted on making the trip with them. Aunt Molly helped them pack and gave them repeated assurances that she would care for the house while they were away. By noon they were ready to start, and at nine o'clock, as Aunt Molly was preparing for bed, a call came from Sherry.

"We came through in fine shape. Kit was in bed in the hospital by four. She has had three shots of penicillin already, and when we left a while ago she was sound asleep. Ginny and I are staying with Jim's ladylove, and Steve is with Jim. As soon as we've seen the doctor in the morning, Steve and I will start for home."

Telling them "good-bye" next morning was an ordeal for Virginia. She felt as if some badly-needed props were being withdrawn from her. She had not realized how closely her life had become knit to these friends until she had to see them depart while she stayed behind in the city that had become an almost alien place to her. After Sherry had gone out to the car Steve returned for a final word.

"Don't worry, dear," he said, apparently not realizing that he had used the term of endearment. "Dr. Sawyer told Jim and me that he is very confident that the infection can be permanently overcome. This is just a slight flare-up and will soon be licked. When we get home, Aunt Molly and I will be praying together for you. I want you to call me every day so that I will know not only about Kit, but also about Kit's brave big sister. Don't forget. And keep looking up!"

Did anyone ever have such friends? With them behind her she could go on!

Dr. Sawyer was very happy over the opinions of the other doctors. They all agreed that the infection was localized and could be rather quickly eliminated. There need be no long period of convalescence nor the use of cane or crutch. Two weeks under treatment and observation should be sufficient.

It was on the last day of their stay, when Kit was walking around the hospital and making great plans for the trip in Jim's car next day, that Mr. Hudson came back from a trip to Mexico with the word that unless some unexpected complication should arise Mother and Dad would leave Mexico in two weeks. Reservations had been made in a New York hospital, and as quickly as possible Dad would undergo another operation which, they hoped, would determine the cause of that strange coma in which he lay— determine it and correct it.

It was decided that Jim should go on to New York and meet them in order that Mother should not be alone for the ordeal. After much discussion of the subject they agreed that the situation at home must be frankly told to Mother. Kit was well on the road to complete recovery and Mother would not have the strain and worry of those weeks when the outcome seemed doubtful. After Dad's operation (they did not let themselves consider the eventuality of its not being successful), plans must be made for his and Mother's return. The house on Monterey Boulevard was rented until October. That had seemed best, for by signing a lease for a year they had obtained a much higher rental, so the Martin family would have to live on the farm until then.

"I'll be relieved to have Mother know it," said Virginia as they drove along the highway later in the day. "The secrecy has been one of the hardest parts of it all. Every letter I have written has seemed shallow and insincere. I'm eager to write a *real* letter to Mother. I want her to know Aunt Molly and Sherry and Steve even before she gets here. I think I'll start a letter tonight and make it a book by the time she arrives!"

"Oh, I will, too!" cried Kit. "I want to tell her how we're going to find Allie May, and about the dog I think Steve is going to get for me, and about stoves in place of a furnace, and about the smelly lamps and the organ I pump with my feet. I'll tell her about how good Steve is to us, and how much I wish he was my brother—"

"Oh, do stop for breath," pleaded Virginia hastily.

Jim, glancing at her flushed face, queried laughingly, "Why the blushes? Has the country lawyer replaced the city prof in your—shall we say 'friendship'?"

"Each of my friends has a place of his own," she answered testily. "They don't *have* to replace someone else."

"But sometimes they do. *I* wouldn't grieve if Steve replaced Howard Willis. I never liked that would-be intellectual. I hope you're not carrying a torch for him!"

"Indeed I'm not! He's going to marry Rae Terrant next summer and I'll gladly give them my heartiest best wishes. I meant it when I told you the other day that I didn't feel a bit bad when I met him. I'm not grieving in the least, Jimmie. Not about that."

"About something else? Can I help? We don't stop being pals, do we, just because I've got me another girl?"

"Of course not. I've missed you a lot and I'm glad for this ride that gives me a chance to talk to you. Do you remember the night last August when Dr. Connor preached the sermon on sacrificing ourselves willingly?"

"Yes. I'll never forget it. Dot and I talk about it a lot. It changed things for us. We aren't ready to tell of our plans yet for they aren't thoroughly crystallized. Just now my family problems have to come first. But our future prospects were turned upside down by that sermon. We'll tell you about it when we know definitely what God's will for us is."

"I'm glad for you! I knew that both you and Kurt stood, and I've been wondering how it had or would affect your lives. Dot and I have had almost no time alone since I came up to the city, and most of our talk has been of wedding plans. I'm glad that sermon meant something to you. It must be wonderful to plan your future with some one 'of like mind'."

"It is. I keep thinking of how good God is to give such a great happiness at a time when I needed it so desperately. There's no denying that this winter has been *tough*."

He spoke diffidently, for they had not been accustomed to speak easily of spiritual things. Virginia's answer came quickly.

"Of course it has. I've known that I wasn't carrying *all* the load. You've had a tremendous job, shouldering the responsibility of the family and Dad's office and living in that six-by-nine room at the lab."

"I don't live there." He grinned. "I just go there occasionally to sleep and change clothes. I really live at the Blackwells'. I'm ashamed to hang out there so much, but I can't seem to help it. But let's talk about you. Why did you ask about that night? What did it mean to you?"

"It meant so much that when I had to make a decision

about Kit I felt that was my call to sacrifice. It was a real sacrifice, too, Jimmy. None of you knew how much my work meant to me, and how much it still means. I did like Howard Willis more than I was willing to admit. But that doesn't bother me now. Maybe my standards of manhood have changed. I know I would never have grown to love him as a person should love the mate God intends for him—not as Mother loves Dad or as you love Dot."

"Or as you love the country lawyer?"

"Steve?" said Virginia in amazement, glancing toward the back seat and noting with relief that Kit was asleep with her head pillowed on her suitcase. "Why, I've never thought of love in connection with Steve. He's been the kindest friend one could desire, but he's *just* a friend."

"Then why the blushes?"

"You know why. You can always make me blush just by looking at me. Ever since I've been knee high you've done that to me, and you know it!"

"True, my pal. Many a time you took punishment deserved by me because you looked so guilty. For that I apologize. But I am not quite convinced on the subject of Steve. Anyway, I'm glad about your attitude toward Howard Willis. I was afraid he had hurt you."

"He didn't hurt me permanently. The friendship died before it had time to ripen into anything deeper. But one thing does hurt, Jimmy. That was what I wanted to talk about."

"The job?"

"Yes. I love teaching. It wasn't my first choice as a life-work—at least not teaching English. But when I couldn't go to Clearwater but had to take City College, where they had no real music department, I chose teaching English as my career, and I think I made good!"

"You did. Mr. Blackwell said the other day that Superintendent Hamlin told the board you were the best teacher they had ever had in that department."

"Really? I'm glad. That helps a lot. But that won't save my job. Howard Willis is the new principal, and his wife will want the position—and she will get it. Even if I wanted to go back (which I don't under the circumstances), he wouldn't want to be embarrassed by my presence. I would probably be sent to head up the work at junior high. A year ago I would have been elated at that. Now it would definitely seem a demotion."

"That's a rotten deal! They know you were on leave because of Kit's illness."

"I know it. But even that isn't bothering me now. The question that comes to me, and I've wondered about it a lot in the last few weeks, is the why of it all. I mean—why was the work I loved taken away from me? I was doing well in it, and after Dr. Connor gave us that sermon I gave my work to God, thinking that it was my way of serving Him. I thought I could be an inspiration to my boys and girls. A thoroughly consecrated teacher has a wonderful opportunity to show her Master to her scholars. Why, then, did I have to give it up? Why do I have to be buried in a tiny village, building fires, cleaning lamps and washing dishes? Am I not yet fit to serve Him? What is He trying to teach me?"

"I don't know. One thing you said just now is worth thinking about, however. You said that you gave your work to God. Then it is His, isn't it, to do with as He sees fit. This winter I've been learning that I'm not my own and that my Master has the right to use me and my life as He deems best. I must not even question."

"I know that's right and true. But none of us wants to be thrown away as useless scrap. And that's what I seem to be."

"You're wrong! The One who died for you will never discard you. Maybe it seems to you that you are counted as scrap. But I am inclined to believe that God saw something especially promising in you and is just polishing you a bit to make you more fit for service."

"You're sweet, Jimmy, and a wonderful comfort. No wonder Dot thinks you are a honey. You are! I'm not always so gloomy. But having made my sacrifice, I guess I want to see a few results."

"I could name a few. Kit has been helped back to strength
again, Kurt has been kept in school, Mother and Dad have
been kept from the worry of our problems, and I'm sure
Aunt Molly and Sherry Carlson have been helped—not to
mention the sunshine you've brought into Steve Barrett's
life."

"Now you're trying to be funny. I'll admit some of the
things you mention. But I'm afraid you'll have to cross Sherry
off the list. The good I've done her, if any, is purely phy-
sical. She's had a shelter, but perhaps if she hadn't had it
she would have returned to her parents and brother. That's
where she should be, and maybe my help has just encouraged
her in her willfulness."

"She must be a sweet character. Sorry I didn't meet her."

"She can be charming, when she wants to be. And she can
be just the opposite. But I love her very much. I would
consider this winter worth while if I could lead Sherry to
Christ. But we've talked ourselves hoarse and she just laughs
at us. Or else she slams out of the room and won't speak
to us for hours. I get *so* discouraged about her."

"Maybe you talk too much."

"That's what Aunt Molly says. But it's hard to keep still.
Sometimes I think she tries to provoke us to argument. Other
times she says she won't talk about it. That's why I feel so
low, I guess. I get no results from the only piece of witnessing
I ever did. I was willing to be a sacrifice. But I don't want
to be a useless one!"

"I don't think any sacrifice will ever be a useless one
Ginny. I believe you'll win Sherry yet."

He told her of his own recent experience and gave her
the Scripture that had helped him. As they turned into the
lane that led to the old farmhouse under the maple trees,
Virginia said, "Thanks a lot, Jimmy. I needed a talk with
you. I'm back on the job again and I'll win out. Sherry just
has to believe!"

Chapter Twenty

Kit had her head bent over the table and was laboriously writing thank-you notes to friends who had been kind to her during her "incarceration," as Sherry called it. Kit rather doubted whether the kindness had been worth such great effort as she was now expending, but Virginia had said that these notes must be ready for today's mail. If they weren't Virginia would call Steve and tell him not to bring the puppy he had promised. All were finished except the one to her bosom friend, Fran. She was making a real letter of that.

"I've told her that Daddy is better and that he and Mother will be in New York soon. I'm telling her now about the doctor that—that came from—from—" She consulted Mother's last letter. "Ginny, how do you pronounce Q-u-i-t-o?"

"You don't have to pronounce it," said Sherry. "Just write it."

"I know that." Kit laughed. "But it's such a queer name. That's where the doctor that's traveling with the folks, came from. How do you pronounce it, Ginny?"

"It's not hard. Divide it this way: Q-u-i pronounced 'key', then t-o pronounced 'toe.'"

"Well, that's a silly way to spell it. I'd spell it K-e-e-t-o-w."

Kit continued with her letter-writing, not noticing the startled expression on her sister's face. Aunt Molly was too occupied with her darning to be aware of anything unusual. Virginia stood for a moment as if unable to move, then ran to the telephone. Her hand was shaking so that she could scarcely hold the receiver to her ear.

"Oh, Steve, I'm so glad you were in! No, everything's all right, but I'm so excited that I'm afraid I can't talk rationally. Is there a place called 'Quito' in this or a near-by state? Well, can you find out? Listen, Steve, how would a ten-year-old spell 'Quito'?"

She listened for a moment, then, from his gasp, knew that he had comprehended the cause of her excitement.

"I'll go to the post office and locate all the Quitos in the country," he said. "I think we have our teeth in something at last."

Investigation showed that there were five towns of that name in the United States, and to each Steve sent his advertisement. Virginia's name was used this time in the hope that someone seeing it would know that it was a person who loved her who was seeking Allie May.

"Don't you think, now, that we are going to find her before Dad comes?" said Kit, feeling that she had been the heroine of this adventure.

"We hope so," answered Steve. "We have a clue at least and that is more than we've ever had."

So they waited and hoped, watching each day for the mailman and listening all day long for the telephone to ring. But the days passed and no letters or calls came through. At the end of a week, Virginia's optimism began to fade.

"It's just another dream that didn't come true," she told Steve wryly, as they sat before the fire on a gray day. "I shouldn't have let myself become so sure of success. Even if we found that fifteen years ago the Ormands lived in or near one of those Quitos, that's no assurance that they still do or that they would let anyone know their whereabouts if they moved on. If they moved and left no address once, they could do it again. I'm going to quit thinking about it."

"Well, I'm not," asserted Kit. "I'm going to keep on praying and believing that Allie May will come back to us. I'm not going to quit doing that any more than I'm going to quit believing that Steve will *someday* bring me a little dog!"

With a startled exclamation Steve started from his chair. "Come out to the car, Kit, and see what I have in the back seat. That is, I hope the back seat is still there and intact."

They returned in a few minutes with Kit proudly clasping a white puppy in her arms.

"He's mine! He's *all* mine! Steve said so. Oh, I *knew* I'd have a dog someday! And I know we'll find Allie May, too, Ginny. I do! Isn't he a beautiful dog, Ginny? He's a genuine—er—er—"

"Dog," supplied Sherry. "Just dog. That's the best kind."

"This chap has been taught to behave himself and leave the furniture and curtains alone. I'll guarantee his good behavior," Steve assured.

"Has he been taught to keep a proper distance from hosiery?" asked Virginia anxiously.

"If he hasn't, he can soon learn." Sherry patted the head of the puppy and reassured Kit. "Let me help you teach him. I'm an expert at handling dogs."

As Virginia watched her working patiently and understandingly with the puppy and the little girl, she felt again a surge of love for the temperamental, hard-to-understand Sherry. Somehow she *must* win Sherry to Christ!

"I feel about that as Kit does about Allie May. I can't give up," she said to Steve and Aunt Molly later when Sherry had taken Kit and the pup for a ride in Steve's car. "If I could get her to really talk seriously once, at a time when we would not be interrupted, I think she would listen."

As the days passed, however, Virginia became discouraged. However, the prayed-for opening came unexpectedly.

"What's the matter with you two soul-winners?" Sherry asked sarcastically as they were clearing the table after Sunday dinner. "I used to think that Steve hung around here so much because he was trying to be a good influence for me. Now I'm beginning to think he just likes my cooking. He's just another unsatisfied appetite. Men! Bah!"

"Did you like me better when I was trying to convert you?"

"Well, life was a bit more interesting then, at least. Now Ginny keeps her nose in a book all the time, and you haven't been near us for several days. Maybe you've found yourself a girl friend and are giving her the joy of your fellowship while we sit deserted. Oh, for a real argument once more!"

"Do you mean that?"

"Certainly. I'm getting a case of the screaming meemies just sitting around here."

"O.K., my dear cousin, we will accommodate. To avoid any unpleasantness spilling over on poor Aunt Molly, let's go down to her house for our little debate. I have to take some measurements for the carpenter, anyway."

Before they left, Virginia went to her room and knelt beside her bed.

"Oh, Lord," she prayed. "Show me what to say. I feel so ignorant when I am talking to Sherry. But You can help me, and I need You so much. Soften her heart and convince her of Your truth."

When Steve had built a fire in the stove and the room had begun to grow warm after its weeks of frigidity, the three of them seated themselves on the sofa, Sherry in the middle and Steve and Virginia at either end.

True to her promise she gave them her full attention. It was a serious hour to them—an hour for which they had prayed and studied to the limit of their ability. One by one they gave their proofs to her, proofs that the Bible was, in truth, God's Word. They cited its unity, its fulfilled prophecies, its permanence, its superior teaching, its proved promises, its unfailing strength, its comfort for the saints of all ages.

For over an hour they talked, and Sherry listened gravely. Occasionally she would question some statement or correct a faulty bit of logic. When they paused she spoke slowly, as if without interest in the subject.

"I suppose that all those arguments are true—at least as true as we can know anything to be. I haven't any arguments, against them. Oh, I know what skeptics and atheists say. I've read a lot of that stuff. But your views are more tenable, for you admit that it's all beyond reason, and that's what God has to be to be God at all. And I know that the Bible could not be the product of man's unaided intellect. So I won't dispute your ideas. I'll just say I can't accept them."

"How can you say that you suppose that they are true, and yet not accept them?" Virginia spoke in a troubled and puzzled tone.

"I guess my head admits it all but my heart refuses to fall into line. It isn't real belief unless it comes from the heart, is it?"

"No."

"Let's just say that I have no heart, or if I have a bit of one left, it refuses to be involved."

"But, listen, Sherry," pleaded Virginia, "you know your Bible as well as we do, so you can understand this. God made man in His own image and gave him a wonderful and beautiful world to live in. Man fell into sin and was completely alienated from God. God, being God, could not look on sin. All mankind partook of that sin. I was reading in Romans yesterday, 'By one man sin entered into the world, and death by sin; and so death passed upon all men, for that all have sinned.' They've sinned and 'come short of the glory of God.' Oh, Sherry, you can't deny that you've come short of *that!*"

"Hardly," answered Sherry grimly. "In my most exalted moments I've never claimed to have attained to 'the glory of God.' "

"Don't you see, then, that you need Chirst?"

Sherry did not answer, and Steve took up the plea.

"God could not look on sin. The gulf between Him and man was so great that man could never bridge it. The sin of the world was so black that it *had* to be punished. The debt to God was so great that it *had* to be paid. No man was sufficient to pay it. Only God Himself could do it. So Jesus Christ, God's only Son, His only begotten Son, came to die

for us. It was no man that died that day. It was 'very
God of very God'! Some folks want to deny that sonship, but
I can't believe that anyone who has really felt the weight of
sin on his soul could believe that any man could atone for
it."

"I wouldn't deny His sonship," said Sherry. "If I believed
at all, I'd believe it all."

"Can't you see?" pleaded Virginia. "Can't you see your need
of a Saviour and God's provision of one? Can't you believe
that?"

Sherry sat, unanswering. Until the fire had died and
the shadows began to creep into the room, they talked to
her. But she kept that dull apathy that was harder to meet
than her former stormy opposition. At last she rose, saying
abruptly, "You are two faithful witnesses to your faith all
right. I won't tease you any more. I admire you for your
zeal and steadfastness. If I *could* believe I'd be glad to. But
I can't seem to get up a whit of feeling about it. Such
heart as I might have had once has been battered into
unconsciousness."

She went from them and they stared at each other in
dismay.

Chapter Twenty-One

Events happened so swiftly that first week in March that the folks in the old gray house could scarcely keep up with them. In Monday's mail came an answer to Virginia's advertisement. Mrs. Alice Martin and her daughter Allie May and her parents, Mr. and Mrs. Neil Ormand, had lived on a farm about six miles from Quito which was less than three hundred miles from them. They had left some eight years ago after the death of the older folks, and the writer did not know where they now were. But this information was enough to send Steve to Quito as fast as his car could carry him. With that much to go on they could surely find out more! Virginia's hopes rose again. Perhaps they would have good news for Dad after all!

Then on Tuesday, after Steve had gone, Jim telephoned from the city. The plane carrying their parents was scheduled to arrive in New York on Saturday, and he would be on hand to meet it. He would call them from New York as soon as possible and would keep them informed about the operation and Dad's condition.

"The Blackwells and the Connors and all the folks at church said to tell you they're praying with us Ginny. Can't you feel the Arms underneath?"

"Yes. And don't you worry about us, Jim. We'll carry on and wait for you."

When Virginia turned from the phone she was shaking as if with a chill.

"I don't see how I can live through these next few days,

Aunt Molly. Jim was so sure and quiet, but I get sick when I think what it all may mean to us."

The old lady reached out and with her brown hands held Virginia's trembling ones until they became quiet.

"'In quietness and confidence shall be your strength'" she said. "You have carried your load so long that you feel weak at the thought of losin' it. The way to meet these days is to fill 'em with work. If tomorrow's as warm as today, let's get the blankets out on the line to air. Nothin' like a March wind to freshen things up!"

"All right, we'll clean house," said Virginia, drawing a long breath. "I'll wash and iron the parlor and dining-room curtains. Even in the country, curtains are dirt-catchers!"

So they swept and dusted and aired bedding and laundered blankets. Sherry and Kit appointed themselves window-washers, and with Sherry on the outside and Kit on the inside they washed and polished until the glass shone.

Sherry had been nervous and unhappy for days. She took an unusual number of long walks into the woods or the village. She was the first to get the mail each day and asked anxiously and often if Steve had been heard from. Virginia felt that some crisis had arisen in the unhappy girl's affairs.

But when, on Friday evening, Steve drove in, she did not greet him with enthusiasm. Virginia and Kit made up for her lack, however, for they were out on the porch to meet him before the car had stopped. One look at his face made Virginia's heart sink. He met her gaze over Kit's head, and shook his own.

He spoke soberly. "I'll come in and tell you what little I know before I go home and clean up. I'm as tired and dirty as the proverbial dog."

"You're going to stay for supper," said Virginia, drawing him inside. "We aren't even going to ask you any questions until you've washed and eaten. Go up to the east room and clean up while we get supper on. Here's hot water and there are towels on the rack."

It was across the table that he told his story. He had found the farm where the Ormands had lived for a number of years. He had talked to the man who had bought the farm after Neil Ormand died. He had questioned the neighbors who remembered them. He had visited the Quito High School and talked with several teachers who had been there when Allie May attended.

"She was a charming, naive child," one had said.

"A hoydenish Indian," said another.

But none of them, teachers or neighbors, knew where Allie May and her mother were to be found. One young fellow who had attended State University several years ago insisted he had seen her several times on the campus.

"I know it was Allie May," he said. "I graduated in the same class from Quito High, and used to take her to parties occasionally. I couldn't be mistaken. I didn't talk to her, but once when we met in a hall she nodded to me. It was she, I know."

So Steve had driven up to State University and spent a day there. Three Alice Martins had been enrolled within the last eight years. He had traced them all, and not one of them could have been the one they were seeking.

"So here I am, right back where I started. The elusive Allie May is still eluding me."

"I hadn't let myself hope too much," said Virginia, with a sigh, "so I'm not too disappointed. I don't dare let myself hope that we will find her."

"Well, I *had* hoped, and I *am* disappointed," wailed Kit. "I'm getting tired of being disappointed."

Sherry, whose mercurial spirits had risen, for no apparent reason, said soothingly, "That's too bad, Kitten. But come and see what I have for you. In the drugstore today I found a whole magazine of the dandiest dog pictures. Some of them look just like Doughboy here."

"Oh, goody! I wanted to finish the scrapbook before Daddy got home but I had run out of pictures. Sherry, you're wonderful!"

On Saturday morning the mailman brought a letter that Jim had written on the train.

> Kurt is with me. When the train was about a hundred miles out he came strolling into the car looking like a puppy that had chewed up its boss' best hat. I couldn't send him back. He had spent his own money for a ticket, and had enough for his expenses for a week. Guess I was rather glad to see him, anyway, for I was pretty low. He's a good kid.
>
> We will call after the plane gets in, and again after the operation. Keep a stiff upper lip, pal.
>
> Yours,
> **Jim**

All afternoon they watched the clock. Minute after minute ticked by, and one by one the hours crept away. Sherry did all that she could to enliven the situation and make the time pass more rapidly, but after supper was over and the dishes cleared away, neither Virginia nor Kit could be interested in any game or scrapbook. Even Doughboy was forgotten while they sat tensely waiting. When the phone finally rang they both raced for it. Virginia, being the taller reached the receiver first, but promised Kit she would talk later.

"Hello, Ginny!" came Jim's voice. "All O.K. here. They landed at six-fifteen. Kurt and I went up to the hospital with them. Then when Dad was settled we brought Mom here to the hotel. She said she didn't dare talk to you but for me to tell you she's all right. She's a brick! She's awfully tired, but says she'll sleep better tonight than she has for months."

"Did you see Dad?"

"Yes, for a minute. But he didn't notice us. We'll call again after the operation Monday. Now put Kit up. I have a message for her."

After the message had been delivered Kit turned to them with a shining face.

"My mother and daddy are in the United States!" she cried ecstatically.

Over Sunday the lift in spirits lingered, and Monday afternoon Jim called again to say that the operation was over and although Dad had not regained consciousness the doctors were confident that the difficulty had been discovered and eliminated.

"They won't let Kurt or me see him now, but we'll call again when there's any change."

Aunt Molly and Sherry were as anxious as Virginia and Kit, and kept as close to the phone as their affairs would permit. Steve made Sherry promise to call him the minute any word was received, and each evening when he had closed his office he drove out to wait with them for news.

Each day the word was encouraging as to the patient's general condition. And one evening came Jim's jubilant message.

"He knew her today, Ginny! He said, 'Hello, Marcia. What are you doing here?' The doctor says everything's O.K. now. No, Kurt and I can't see him. There's nothing more for us to do here, so we'll be starting home in a couple of days. Mom wants us to come past and tell you girls all about it before we head back for the city. So we'll be seein' you!"

There was rejoicing in the old house that night. Virginia laid her head on the table and sobbed while Aunt Molly smoothed her hair and spoke words of reassurance and comfort. Sherry reached into Steve's pocket and took his big handkerchief to wipe her eyes, then daubed at the tear on his cheek also, while Kit became so jubilantly excited that Sherry finally gave her a sleeping powder before she could be induced to sleep.

Chapter Twenty-Two

Virginia and Sherry had gone to market, Aunt Molly was down at her cottage looking at the work the carpenters were doing, and Kit was preparing to take Doughboy for a walk when the telephone rang.

"That can't be Jim 'cause he's on the train coming home. I wonder who it is," mused the little girl, as she left Doughboy on the porch and hurried inside. The message came through clearly, and Kit's eyes sparkled as she listened.

"Tell Miss Virginia Martin to call Mr. G. L. Kinder at the Sheridan Hotel in Sparta before five o'clock, if she wants to hear about Allie May Martin."

Kit wrote the name as it was given her, then when she left the telephone wrote a note to Virginia and left it on the table in plain view. This done, she called to Doughboy and went off down the orchard path, and on to Aunt Molly's house. She watched the men at work on the chimney and the roof, and then walked back home with Aunt Molly. As she hung her wraps in the closet she remembered the note.

"Oh, did you call the man, Ginny?"

"What man?"

"The one about Allie May. The one I wrote you a note about."

"What do you mean? I didn't see any note."

"It was right here! Didn't you see it, Ginny? It was about Allie May!" Kit's voice rose high in her fear that the note was lost. "A man called and said for you to call him at a hotel before five o'clock and he'd tell you about Allie May."

"Where did you put the note?"

"Right here on the table. I know I did! Let's look!"

They searched the table and floor thoroughly. They knew that Doughboy was innocent as he had been with Kit all afternoon. The door had not been left open, so no wind could have carried it away. Virginia had come home alone, having parted from Sherry at the church where she had stopped to practice Sunday's anthem. She had put her parcels and music down on the table and was sure there had been no paper on it. The bag of groceries on the kitchen table told them that Sherry had been in, but she was not here now. She must have seen the note if it were there when she came in, but she would not have disturbed it, they were sure. But search as they would they could not find it, and Kit could remember neither the name of the hotel nor the man. Five o'clock drew near and still the search was unavailing. Kit's eyes were tear-filled, for she felt that she had been careless.

When Sherry came in at five-thirty, her quick eye detected the depression on the faces of the girls and the traces of tears on Kit's cheeks. Kit was speaking. "Ginny, I feel so *badly*. It's been a long time since I lost anything. I thought I wasn't a loser any more. I'd rather lose *anything* than that."

Before Virginia could answer, Sherry spoke.

"What's lost now?"

While they told her she looked anxiously, first at Virginia's face, then at Kit's. Putting her arm around the little girl's shoulder, she said kindly, "Don't blame yourself, Kit. I'm afraid I'm the guilty party."

"What do you mean?" asked Virginia sharply. "Did you get it?"

"Well, I must have lost it. Kit says she left it on the table, and I was the first one home after that. I put my parcels here while I went out to the kitchen with the groceries. When I came back I unwrapped the things I had bought and then gathered up the wrappings and burned them. I *must* have taken the note with them."

There was nothing that Virginia could say without disclosing her sick disappointment, so she was silent. Sherry looked at her with frightened eyes, and said falteringly, "I really am sorry, Ginny. I didn't think—"

"Forget it," said Virginia. "There isn't a thing any of us can do. It's past five now, and any chance we had of hearing about Allie May is spoiled, so let's not talk of it."

"Of course it's spoiled!" cried Sherry. "Everything I have anything to do with is always spoiled! The harder I try to do right, the worse messes I get into. Oh, I hate everything— and I hate myself most of all!"

Virginia realized, as she listened to Sherry's outburst, that she had let her disappointment betray her into speaking so sharply that she had hurt her friend whom she wanted only to help.

"Don't Sherry, please! Don't talk so. I didn't mean what I said. We can try again. Please, dear, don't feel so badly."

"I can't help it. You'd feel badly, too, if nothing *ever* went right and if *everybody* always thought you were wrong and bad."

"But *we* don't think so. We know you aren't bad, and we all love you. Come on; let's forget about it."

"I can't and I don't want to. I'm so *tired* of things being wrong. I'm not going to stay here where I can hurt you folks any more. I'm going to leave as soon as I can."

Virginia pleaded with her again to try to forget it all, and to believe that they wanted her. But Sherry clung to her decision to leave.

"There's no train tonight, but I'm going in the morning. And this time even Steve won't know where I am!"

She ran upstairs and neither Virginia's reasoning, Kit's coaxing, nor the smell of Aunt Molly's cornbread could get her to come down. Virginia telephoned for Steve, and he talked to her for an hour, but she refused even to answer him. He came down looking completely defeated.

"This is the end," he said. "I told her I was going to send for her folks, but she'd leave tonight if I did. I'm at my wit's end."

"But not at God's wit's end," said Aunt Molly. "Don't get so bothered. I feel more encouraged about Sherry tonight than I ever have. She wouldn't get riled up so easy unless God was dealin' with her. He'll win out!"

Long after Aunt Molly and Kit had gone to bed, Virginia and Steve sat and talked about their problem. Steve felt that he had failed not only Sherry, but his aunt and uncle and cousin Don.

Virginia spoke. "I have a feeling that she's on the defensive against us—that she doesn't dare trust us fully—that she doesn't believe in our love for her. Oh, if I could only convince her of that! I never had anything mean so much to me in my whole life. It means more than having Daddy get well, because Dad is a Christian. It means more than finding Allie May, much as I want to do that. I think the thing that disturbed her so much this afternoon was the knowledge that she had destroyed the clue that might have led us to Allie May. I was disturbed, too, and I'm ashamed that I let her know it. I'd be willing *never* to find Allie May if I could just convince Sherry of how much I love her, and that, in spite of all her faults, Christ loves her much more than I ever can. Oh, Steve, I'd be willing to die myself if I could convince her!"

"Do you mean that?" came Sherry's tense tones from the doorway. "Ginny, do you *mean* that?"

Virginia and Steve sprang from the davenport and started toward her. She was leaning against the door, and her dark eyes revealed a desperate yearning. Virginia's arms went about her.

"Sherry dear, of course I mean it! If I could only make you believe me! I love you just as you are, and I'd give

anything I possess if I could make you understand that
Jesus loves you much more than I can."

Steve spoke, looking straight into her eyes.

"Sherry, neither Ginny nor I knows just what it is that's
troubling you. We don't know what's keeping you away from
the folks you love and who are now heartbroken over you.
They love you so much that they're sick over separation
from you. But God loves you more than that. We don't know
what sin is keeping you here when your heart is aching for
your folks, but God knows that, too. And He can forgive it
all.'"

Sherry's eyes closed as the tears streamed down her
cheeks.

"How can He care when I've been so stubborn? Will you
two ask Him for me?"

The three of them knelt beside the davenport. Steve, sensing
that Virginia could not speak, prayed first asking the Holy
Spirit to lead Sherry into a knowledge and acceptance of
Christ's redeeming love. Then Virginia prayed, thanking
God for that love and asking that Sherry might realize it.
Both prayers were halting and without smoothness or
polish. But they were sincere and blazed their way to the
Throne. As they prayed, the greatest miracle in the world
took place once more,—a soul was born into the family of
God through faith in the shed blood of His only Son. When
Virginia and Steve had prayed they waited, wondering if
Sherry would offer a petition. With a sob, she began.

"Thank You, Lord. You are the only one who could have
love enough to atone for me. I am Yours forever. Please
help me to do what I have to do now. Amen."

When they arose from their knees, she spoke with typical
decision and thoroughness.

"Steve, will you get the folks on the phone while I wash
my face? I have to talk to them tonight."

By the time Central's voice said, "Here is your party,"
Sherry was ready to talk. Steve reached for Virginia's hand
and gripped it nervously as they waited.

"Hello—hello! Mother, is it you? —Yes, it is. —Oh, Mother, I'm—I'm sorry!"

The voice at the other end of the line must have betrayed its owner's emotions, for Sherry was saying, "Mother, don't cry! Just listen. I'm all changed, Mother—and I—I want to tell you first of all that I'm sorry. Mother—Mother—can you hear me? What? Oh, hello, Dad! Yes, I meant it, and I want to come home! Dad may I talk to Don now?"

As she listened, her face registered disappointment. Then she said firmly, "No, I can't come, Dad, until I talk to Don. Tell him to call me as soon as he gets in tomorrow. Oh, Dad, I do love you all, and I wish Mother could kiss me good night right now!"

She turned from the phone and sat down on a chair as if exhausted.

"Don's out on a buying trip. Dad thinks he'll be back in tomorrow early and he'll call then—I hope."

"You know he will," assured Steve, giving her a reassuring pat on the shoulder.

"If he calls by noon, I'm starting home on the two o'clock train."

At the thought she sat up alertly as if her weariness had vanished. "Ginny, will you set my hair before we go to bed? I want an extra-special hair-do tomorrow. It's going to be my big day, and I want to shine!"

Chapter Twenty-Three

Whil they were eating breakfast next morning,
Sherry decided that only by keeping busy could she live
through the hours until a call came.

"Aunt Molly and Ginny cleaned so hard last week that
there's nothing left for me to clean," she mourned. "Oh,
I know! While the parlor fire is out, I'll polish the stove.
Its shining beauty will give you something to remember me
by when I've left you—which thing I am going to do this
very day, if I can!"

"If you do the best polishin' job that was ever done, it
couldn't shine the way your face does this morning,"
said Aunt Molly happily.

Sherry found stove blacking and brushes in the lumber
room, and, having spread newspapers over the floor to
protect the carpet, she began her labors with Kit as an
admiring audience. Kit had been wakened at seven o'clock
by hearing Virginia tell Aunt Molly what had happened
last night, and her whole day had assumed a roseate glow.
Even the news that Sherry might leave soon did not dim
her joy, for Sherry had promised that she would have Kit
come to visit her in her own home—"the loveliest house, in the
nicest town, with the dearest people in the world." she
said.

She climbed onto a stool and began to work on the pipe.
The stool was low, and even for Sherry's extreme height the
reach was difficult. But the stepladder was out in the
shed and she was in a hurry. She leaned over to polish the

last spot next to the wall. In doing so she stepped too close to the edge of the stool. The stool tipped and Sherry, feeling herself falling, grabbed at the stove pipe. The pipe had not been intended as a support for such a weight, and it and Sherry came down together. Virginia and Aunt Molly heard Kit's scream and the clatter, and came running to find Sherry in the ruins. The pipe had contained several months' accumulation of soot, and this was now liberally sprinkled over Sherry's person.

"Oh!" squealed Kit suddenly from the window, "There's a man running down the lane. Steve's coming, too. And there's a yellow jeep!"

Sherry flew to the window, then whirled with face aglow.

"Oh, get out! Get out, *please!* All of you, *get out!*"

She gave them a shove through the door, slammed it, and left them, a bewildered group in the middle of the dining room. Kit recovered her breath first.

"She just *shoveled* us out!" she sputtered.

Steve knocked at the door, then came in without waiting for an answer, looking excited and happy.

"My guest didn't stop to knock," he said, smiling. "But the emergency was great and I hope you'll forgive him."

"I presume that Sherry's brother has arrived," said Virginia as Kit started a tale of the morning's adventure.

Fifteen minutes later Sherry's voice called, "Steve," and he hurried into the parlor. He was back in a minute.

"I never saw such a sight. Trust Sherry to get into a mess like that. She has gone upstairs to clean up, and wants me to take Don and some hot water up to the east room. She has blacked him up for fair!"

"I'd better take more water up to her," said Virginia. "It will take more than one pitcherful to clean her up. Oh, for a bathtub and unlimited hot water!"

It was an hour later that Virginia and Kit entered the parlor once more. Steve rose to introduce them to the tall young man beside him.

"My cousin, Don Carlson."

Don shook hands with them and seated himself again between Steve and Sherry. One arm was around Sherry's shoulders and she rested trustfully against him. She was a transformed Sherry—eyes shining, cheeks glowing, her face surrounded with brown curls that kept slipping from the red ribbon with which Virginia had attempted to bind them. Gone was the sallow, sullen girl with the absurd topknot. In her place was this radiant young woman who had said last night, "I want to shine!" She was really shining today.

It was into the midst of this happy situation that Jim and Kurt walked. They had six hours before the train must take them on to the city, and they wanted to give their sisters a full account of how things were going at the hospital in New York. As soon as they had been introduced, Sherry and Don slipped out to the kitchen, sending back word by Aunt Molly that they would get lunch and let the brothers and sisters visit.

"No, we didn't see Dad," said Jim. "We stood outside in the hall and heard him talk to Mother. His voice was pretty strong yesterday afternoon."

"Doc says he can come home in about three weeks if all goes well," put in Kurt.

"Home?" said Virginia. "It will have to be here. Kit is well enough now to go upstairs and we'll fix that back bedroom for him. Did you tell Mother all about us, Jim?"

"Yes, and she almost had a fit when she heard about Kit's leg and your living out here. I had a hard time getting her calm enough to go back to Dad."

"Yeah, but she was bustin' her buttons with pride before we left to think her kids could be so smart and self-reliant."

"I don't blame her," said Kit. "I think we're keen! And it's been fun, too!"

"Sez you!" replied Jim, looking over her head at Virginia, who smiled back at him and remarked, "With Dad getting well and Sherry so happy, anything would seem like fun."

"All we need now to complete a full and rounded success

is to find that elusive maiden Allie May Martin," said Jim. "Any new clues, Sherlock?"

"Not too good," said Steve slowly, "but we know now where they moved from here, and eventually we'll go on from there."

"Allie May, here we come!" said Kurt. "And if we ever catch up with you, look out!"

They sat for an hour talking happily of the miracle of the operation and the coming reunion with their parents.

"Mother has lost about ten pounds." said Jim. "Either she didn't like Mexican food or she worried more than she let us know, but she's so happy now that she'll soon regain it. After she got used to the thought, I think she was rather pleased with the idea of just resting here on the farm."

"Resting?" said Virginia sarcastically "What *is* rest?"

"Poor old Ginny!" said Kurt, picking up one of her hands and examining it. "When we're all back in the old home rut again we'll give a dinner in your honor."

"Fine. Will you do the dishes, too?"

"Sure thing. Or Jim will. Maybe Steve will help him."

"I surely will if I'm invited—which reminds me—am I invited for lunch today, or did some one just forget to mention it?"

"Considering the fact that you shot the bear we're serving, you may stay," said Sherry from the doorway. "Come on in. We've stretched the table and there's room for all."

"I gather we're getting one of the hams from Aunt Molly's smokehouse. Bear meat can't touch it."

Throughout the meal Jim gave his attention to Don at his side, glancing often to Sherry just beyond him. Sherry herself was unusually quiet, as a reaction, probably, to the emotional heights that the day had brought. Kurt, across the table from her, wondered at the transformation from his tomboyish pal of a few months ago to this radiant young woman.

Later they all gathered in the parlor again to listen to a concert that Kit presented. As they left the dining room Sherry whispered to Steve. "Don't run out on us yet. I have to say something that you ought to hear."

They all sang, and when they tired of that, they rested and talked. They could not help talking about Dad. It was thrilling just to know he was getting well.

"We stayed behind a screen when he was coming out of ether," Jim told them. "He kept saying 'In the brief case; in the brief case, over and over. Guess he must have had his brief case and its contents on his mind when the crash came."

Aunt Molly's ball of yarn dropped to the floor. Sherry and Don dived for it, bumped heads and came up laughing. Jim looked at them and started to speak, but Aunt Molly was ahead of him.

"That reminds me of when Fred Martin was sick. He never really come to himself after Joe found him by the shed. I come over an' helped take care of him, and' all that night he kep' sayin' 'in the post office; in the post office.' We thought later—"

Her voice was drowned in a sharp exclamation from Jim. He was staring more intently at Sherry, and she had risen to her feet and faced him with wide-open startled eyes. Suddenly he laughed, a great shout of laughter, and crossed the room at one stride to grab her by the shoulders and say, with a chuckle, "Oh oh! What a banty *you* turned out to be!"

While the others sat in stunned silence she stared back, then, as if waking from a dream, cried, "Jimmy! Come on!"

Hand in hand they darted from the room. Across the driveway and over the fence they went, not bothering to open the gate. Don grabbed his leather jacket and started after them, saying, "She'll catch cold."

Kurt and Steve were at his heels, and Virginia and Kit and Aunt Molly hesitated only long enough to get their coats before they, too, hurried across the field. The two ahead had gone to the tree by the creek, and when Virginia came up she could see that Jim, on his knees, was reaching under the bridge. Sherry was standing over him and shaking so violently that Don could scarcely get the coat around her shoulders. Jim was reaching and grunting with the exertion, and it seemed a long time before he drew himself back onto the bank. In his hand was a glass jar so covered with dirt that its contents were not discernible. He tried to open it but the lid was too rusted to turn. Sherry was whimpering against Don's shoulder and now she gasped, "Break it, Jimmy! Break it!"

Jim swung it against the tree and the glass shattered at their feet. Sherry darted forward and picked up the dark object that fell to the ground. Opening it with shaking fingers, she turned toward the others and took a few steps in their direction, crying, "It's there! It is! Oh, Don!"

Before Don could catch her she had fallen white and inert at his feet. Quickly he raised her while Steve and Virginia rubbed her hands and Jim brought his handkerchief, dripping with the cold water of the creek. In a few minutes her eyes opened.

"What's the matter?" she asked, trying to struggle to her feet.

"You blacked out," said Don, "and I'm carrying you to the house right now."

"Oh—I—can walk."

"No, you can't," put in Steve. "Don and I are going to carry you."

"Pretty silly. I can walk."

Nevertheless they did carry her and placed her between them again on the davenport. By that time she was sobbing and it was sometime before she became quiet. When she did, Kurt burst out, "I haven't the foggiest idea what this is all about."

"You tell 'em, Jimmy," said Sherry weakly.

"Well, I hardly know where to begin. The last summer that Ginny and I were here at the farm, Allie May and I had a violent love affair. We wrote love letters to each other and hid them in a niche where the root of the elm tree ran under the bridge. I don't know why we hid them, but we hid them in a glass jar that we pushed into that niche. We didn't think anyone except ourselves knew about it, but I guess Uncle Fred did. And when he got sick that day he put the money in there for safekeeping. I imagine he had seen those tramps about and didn't dare leave it on his person. He knew he was liable to become unconscious.

"Ever since I came here today, Sherry's looks have been bothering me. I thought she must be some girl I met in college. Then when she lost her ribbon and looked so like a cocker spaniel I knew who she looked like, but 1 wasn't sure until she looked so startled when Aunt Molly told that story about the post office. Then I knew she was really Banty."

"The cocker spaniel turned into a gray-hound, Ginny. Didn't I say so?" Sherry laughed shakily.

"But how come Martin has changed to Carlson?" asked Kurt. "The whole thing is as clear as mud to me."

"Simple matter," said Sherry. "I just married this handsome Swede. It's sometimes done, you know!"

They stared in amazement at her. In the excitement of the last half-hour, Virginia had tried to think of some explanation for the change from Allie May Martin to Sherry Carlson, but the simple solution of marriage hadn't occurred to her. Kit was still not satisfied.

"But folks don't change their first names when they get married. If you're Sherry, you can't be Allie May."

Sherry looked up at Don and laughed as she said, "I can explain that, too."

His face flushed and he laughed in embarrassment.

"You see," she said, "my Swede fancies himself a linguist. That is his pronounciation of *cherie*. The day he took me home to his parents (it was a surprise to them) they heard him call me that and thought it was my name. It amused us and we let it stand. Steve visited us that summer and he thought likewise. Allie May hadn't been a very happy girl and I was rather glad to forget her. By the way, that was when Allie May kissed you, Steve."

She laughed at Steve's red face, and continued. "When I went A.W.O.L. and came here to Steve, he introduced me that way, and I let it stand because my real name would have betrayed me, so Sherry I became."

"Well, what does *cherie* mean?" asked Kit.

"In this case it means 'all the world done up in one beautiful bundle,'" said Don, with unexpected fluency.

"What *does* it mean, Ginny?"

"It's French for 'my dear.'"

"Why, I think that's a lovely name. Lots better than Allie May."

"It couldn't be worse," said Sherry. "Don't you remember I said once that Allie May was a silly name?"

"Yes, you did! Did you know all the time—oh, of course you did. *You are Allie May*" Kit was so confused that she could hardly talk.

"What I want to know is this," said Virginia suddenly, "were you in this house that first night we came here?"

"I certainly was. I didn't know you were coming, and I was going to hunt for the money. If you hadn't come, Steve would never have known I was here. But when you turned up I had to have a place to stay, so I hunted up my dear cousin."

"Were you in the house when we came?"

"Yes, but I didn't know you at first. I was peeking out of the south bedroom window when you unloaded. I didn't know you, but I recognized Jim."

"Of course," put in Jim. "No gal ever forgets her first love."

"I hid in the upstairs until Jim and Steve left. I intended to catch the four-thirty train to the city, for your coming had spoiled my plans to search the house. But you almost caught me in the hall and I didn't have a chance to get away until after the train had gone. So I stayed all night. I had to get away before light so I slipped down the back stairs about four o'clock. I felt half starved so I took a bowl of cereal. I was going to wash my bowl and put things away and leave a dime on the table, but you got up for something and I had to leave on the double-quick. I walked over to Grandpa Neil's old granary and hid there until after train time. Then I presented myself at Steve's office. By that time I had recovered my determination to search the house and I intended to find some way to stay here. Steve thought of me only as his cousin's runaway wife, and never realized that the idea of staying with you was being planted in his dear head. I planted it and watered it until it brought forth the desired fruit, and he never once suspected that he was being managed."

Everyone laughed, and Jim said, with a pitying look at Don, "Quite a job you have ahead of you, Mr. Carlson! Being the husband of Allie May is bound to be an interesting vocation."

"Not from now on," said Sherry soberly. "I'm going home to Mother and Dad Carlson and I'm going to show them that I am truly a 'new creation in Christ.' That's all I want to do. It's been lots of fun getting acquainted with you all, and someday I hope you'll all visit us and let me show you what a model wife and housekeeper I can be."

Then she added hastily, "But don't come right away. I want to practice first!"

"One of the funniest sights you ever saw must have been the sight of me chasing Allie May Martin when I had her in my grasp!" said Steve.

"You were a funny old lamb," she said, patting his arm.

"Thanks. That will help a lot to soothe my injured pride. You certainly took me for a ride, but I wasn't completely stupid. I never suspected that Don's wife was Allie May, but I knew you had decided on the Martin farm as your place of residence as soon as you mentioned 'that old gray house out on the highway beyond the creek.' I thought you liked it because of its isolation. But what I want to know now is how you eluded me. Were you at State U. when that chap said you were?"

"Yes, but not as a student. I was working in the office while Don did some postgrad work. But I was not Alice May Martin then. I was Mrs. Alice Carlson. Don and I had finished at Bayside, a little college that Steve failed to investigate, the year before, and he wanted to get in a year at State. So we were married that summer and lived in a trailer. It was fun, wasn't it, Don? You can be very sure that I was careful to avoid Dick Baines after I found out he was there. I had burned all my bridges and I didn't want anyone to remind me of them—at least, not until I found that money and told the world about it!"

"How did you send that letter I got? It was postmarked in a little town in Texas. I almost decided to go down there and look for you. Then I figured you'd played some trick on me."

"I sent it to a friend whose husband is a traveling man. He mailed it for me."

"Why didn't you want us to find you?" reproached Virginia. "We all felt terrible, and Daddy was heartbroken."

"Poor Uncle Lee! He was always so good to me. I guess I wasn't thinking about how bad anyone else felt. I had too much trouble of my own."

"But no one believed—"

Sherrys face was sober and her chin quivered as she spoke again. "I'd better tell it all and get it over with. I don't remember everything. Mother tried to make me forget it. I heard all the awful things that my grandfathers said to each other. It was a terrible thing for a child to go through. It seemed to change them from the grandpas I had loved into fearful old ogres. I wish I had understood then how sorry they both would be afterward. I had thought they were almost perfect, and to see them change so frightened me almost to death. In the years that followed I couldn't forget it.

"Aunt Molly's stories about Grandpa have helped a lot to take that sting away. She helped me to see that even strong Christians like Grandpa and Grandpa Neil were can fall into sin and that God can forgive and restore them to Himself. From what she said about Grandpa and how he grieved I know that Grandpa Neil was doing the same. We heard that Grandpa was dead, and after that, Grandpa Neil was so quiet and sad that we thought he was sick. Both he and Grandma died when I was about fourteen. I am so glad that Aunt Molly told those stories because ever since then I've been remembering my grandfathers as they used to be on these farms. And those stories gave me hope that God might forgive me, too. But it· was Ginny's love that broke me all up in little pieces!"

She stopped for a minute and wiped her eyes with Don's handkerchief. Then she continued, shakily.

"My mother died the year I was a freshman at Bayside and I felt awfully alone. I wanted to come back and be a Martin again, but I had resolved not to do it until I found the money. I didn't need the money for I have all of Grandpa Neil's property, but I did need to clear up the misunderstanding. I *knew* that money was on this farm somewhere! I think I would have quit college, much as I loved it, except that Don came along that year and I sort of forgot everything else.

"But last fall when I went clear off the beam, I decided to come here and try again. I didn't tell Don where I was going and I wouldn't let Steve tell him where I was. I was furiously angry and hurt and I was sure that even Don couldn't love such a person as I knew myself to be. It's awful to think how downright ornery a person can get when he's running from God.

"Steve knew I was here and Don knew I was Allie May and if they'd ever gotten together my goose would have been cooked! The time Steve came home and said he'd seen the folks I was scared stiff! But Steve didn't tell where I was and Don kept my secret, though I was doing my best to break his heart. He's—oh, Don you're a honey. She pulled his head down and kissed him full on the mouth, to his delighted embarrassment.

Kit's eyes had filled with sympathetic tears during this recital, but she was not yet completely satisfied.

"What about your little ring, Sherry—Allie May?" She corrected herself.

"Let it go at 'Sherry'. We're all used to that now. When Uncle Lee gets well I want to come back and see him and be Allie May for awhile. But you folks were mighty good to Sherry, and Don loves her, though I don't see how he can, so I'll be Sherry if you don't mind. Oh—the ring! That was silly. I lost it before Daddy died. Then, when we were hunting for the money, I found it in a crack in a dresser drawer, and lost it again that very day before I could put it away. I knew it was in the bedroom but Ginny wouldn't go away and give me a chance to retrieve it, and Kit found it. May I *please* have it, Ginny?"

When it was brought she handled it lovingly. It was too small for her to wear so she gave it to Don to keep for her.

"I'll get you a watch and chain when you get to be an alderman or something", she promised, "and you can hang that ring where a Phi Beta Kappa key would hang if either of us had ever had such a thing."

The afternoon was growing late and Jim and Kurt began to talk of leaving. That reminded Sherry and Don of their own departure.

"When do we start for home, Don? Can I drive the Yellow Peril?"

"You can if you won't go too fast. I'd like to start now for the folks will be anxious till we get there. But I drove all night and I need some sleep. I've never figured out how to sleep confortably in a jeep, especially with you driving."

Sherry stared at him in amazement. "Why, you poor dear! Where were you?"

"I was over three hundred miles from here. Dad was so excited when you called last night that he couldn't sleep until he had located me. He knew approximately where I was, so he kept calling hotels until he found me. I started at once. That's all."

"Well, I'm taking you upstairs and putting you to bed. You need a nap before supper. I'm going to sit by your side and just gloat over you!"

They started from the room, but Sherry ran back to where Aunt Molly was sitting in the rocker, her old face almost transfigured with joy.

"I've got to give you one big hug and kiss and call you 'lil Aunt Mauwy' like I used to. It's been on my lips a thousand times." Then, looking around the circle, she cried, "I'm going to kiss every one of you. It's been so *long* since I had any folks of my own!" She kissed Ginny last. "I've saved you till last because you're the one who said she'd be willing to die herself if she could lead me to Christ. You'll always have a special place in my heart. That was what made me realize a little bit of what Christ's love is."

Sherry stood for a moment looking at them, her eyes shining and a smile on her lips. Then she turned to Don, and with his arm about her they went up the stairs.

Chapter Twenty-Four

It was late that night. Don and Sherry had retired that they might be ready for an early start next day. Aunt Molly was asleep also, and Virginia had just succeeded in getting Kit to stop talking and relax. As she came into the parlor, Steve rose from the chair where he had been waiting and said, "I think it's time I left, too. Don't you want to go for a ride? I have an errand in Sparta. The man I want to see won't get in until eleven, so we would have just about time to make it. What say? Will you come along?"

"I'll be glad for a spin in the fresh air. It has been such an exciting day that I don't feel I can sleep."

They drove past Aunt Molly's little house under the hill. In another week the workmen would be done and Aunt Molly could go home.

"Just in time, too. She'll begin to put in her garden soon."

On they went. down the road that lay like a ribbon before them in the moonlight. The wind, carrying a promise of spring, came through the window and lifted Virginia's hair.

"Cold?"

"No. I like it. It unties the knots in my nerves."

"It's been a fast twenty-four hours, hasn't it?"

"Yes. This time last night Sherry had not yet found the Lord. First she found Him; then she was reconciled to her family; then Jim and Kurt came with their good news; and then we found the money and Allie May. What a day!"

"A full day and a satisfying one. Before she went to

172

bed Sherry came and apologized again for all the trouble she had caused me. That in itself is a sign that she is changed. I doubt if she ever apologized to anyone in all her life."

"She came to me, too, and told me about burning that note Kit left. She recognized the name as that of an acquaintance who knew of her marriage to Don, so she burned it to keep me from calling him. Then she was so sorry that she was almost sick when I felt so badly. Yet she wasn't willing, even then, to tell us who she was. It was only when Christ came in that her pride and stubborn willfulness went out."

"I wonder why she didn't tell us last night that she was Allie May."

"She told me that, too. It's perfectly logical. To her, the big problem of her life was getting hold of Don. She didn't want to get into the Allie May complications until she had Don at her side to help her face whatever was coming. She was just getting ready to tell us when Jim and Kurt came. Then there was so much confusion that she had no opportunity until Jim recognized her."

"I believe she's happier tonight than in all the years since her father died."

"Probably happier than *ever* before, for the happiness of childhood is an untried thing that can be shattered by circumstances. The happiness that is on her face now is that which comes after triumph over circumstances. I hope you understand what I mean. I'm not saying it very well."

"I think you said it perfectly. Now tell me something else. What about Virginia Martin? What about her happiness? I know you're full of joy over Sherry, but you have your own problems, too, that deserve consideration."

"What—what do you mean?"

"Well, the Virginia who came here last fall was a very brave and unselfish but a very unhappy girl. Has that situation changed? The winter has been a pretty profitable one for most of us, but what about Ginny?"

She waited so long to answer that he said, "Don't tell if you don't want to. I've no right to ask."

"I'd *like* to talk about it. I believe you'll understand better than anyone else because you've seemed to sense the struggles when the others didn't. I was just hesitating a bit to evaluate the gains—and losses, if any."

"*Are* the gains greater than the losses, then?"

"Much, in every way. But it was a long time before I found that out. Until I did it was very hard."

"I know. I watched you fight—and win. Even though I didn't know all that was troubling you, I could sympathize and pray."

"You're the biggest thing I gained this winter—a friend who can watch and pray."

Steve's hand gripped the wheel and he started as if to speak, but Virginia went on.

"I'd like to tell it all to you now. It doesn't hurt any more, and if you'd care to listen, I'd like you to know it all. You helped so much in the fight that you ought to know what the enemies were."

She told him the whole story of the tumbled blocks of a frustrated four-year-old, of the plans and disappointments of the succeeding years, of the most ambitious plan and the greatest disappointment. This was the first time she had put so much into words. Even to Jim she had not bared her hurt as she was doing now. As she spoke, she realized, with a fullness of comprehension, that there was no longer pain or heartache. Even when she spoke of her work she did it with a complete absence of regret.

"Will you believe me, Steve, when I say I don't care a bit about any of it now? I don't know what God has ahead for me, but this winter has taught me to trust Him. I guess that's about the greatest thing I gained—even greater than a dependable and understanding earthly friend. Those two things alone make it a very profitable time."

"Thank you for telling me so much. I know that you

will never be disappointed in your Best Friend. And I hope the other one will be faithful also."

"I'm not worried. He has already stood by so many times when I needed him that I can't doubt him."

"Tell me about the other gains. Are they deep, dark secrets?"

"Well, there's Sherry. I still can't think of her as Allie May. The little cousin whom I cherished was a little spark-plug that kept the whole family pepped up and full of joy. The Sherry that lay on my heart so heavily all winter was such an unhappy person. Yet, as I look back, I can see that there were lots of flashes of our Banty. She never could have become so dear to me under easier circumstances, so I feel that she is one of this winter's rich gains. I can't help thinking of Daddy. I hope Mother doesn't tell him about her until he gets home. I want to see the joy in his face when we tell him.

"Then there's Aunt Molly. There isn't any way to evaluate her. I can't think of life without her. She has taught me lessons in Christian living that will be remembered as long as I live. And the little sermons she preaches to us when we have our Bible readings each morning are better than the finest ones I've heard from any pulpit. I don't mean that they are well organized or—or—homiletically correct. (I believe that's the word I want.) The things she's said have stayed with me and become a part of me and will make me a better Christian."

"I'm glad to have you appreciate Aunt Molly. From the time my mother died when I was a little fellow she has meant more to me than anyone else—even my father. I always spent my summers at her house, and my morals and manners are a direct result of her teaching," Steve said gently.

"I think it was she who taught me the big lesson that stands out above all the others that I have learned this winter. It was not quilting or bread-baking or even how to keep cheerful under such adverse circumstances as smoking lamps and cranky pumps, though those things are valuable and will make me an easier person to live with. It was something unspeakably bigger. As I told you, I've always wanted to do something that would remain after I had passed on. I couldn't bear to live and die and leave behind me nothing of permanent value. That was why I was so depressed about the loss of my job. It was the loss of my great opportunity.

"Then I met Aunt Molly. And I saw her, day by day, living in a way that would leave a permanent impression even on eternity. I've put together things that she said, and things that you and Mr. Harnish and the minister and the storekeepers and others said, and I've learned that from the proceeds of her farm she has kept her nephew and his family in Africa, and has sent several other nieces and nephews into Christian service. She has taught in the Sunday school for over fifty years, and the minister told me that he had never known a person to stay in her class six months without becoming a Christian. She gave wonderful comfort by the stories she told us of Grandpa's life. She showed me how, in spite of his weakness and the mistakes that we know he made, he stood out as a man of God.

"That is the way God has answered all the prayers I have sent up for His blessing on my plans and purposes. He made me discard the plans and change the purposes, and He showed me that the best, the only way to bear lasting fruit for the years to come is to live completely for Christ and witness for Him to others."

They were coming into Sparta, and soon were at the hotel where Steve had his appointment. While he was inside, Virginia sat in the car and thought about the events of the day and the promise of the days ahead. Sherry's problems were solved. Kit was well. Dad and Mother would soon be home. She did not know what lay ahead of her. Would she go back to Claremont, or would some other place of service open? Would they sell the farm and so close all doors on this dear place where she had lived and suffered and fought and triumphed? Was the pain in her heart only from the realization that she must leave the farm in a few months, or was it from the fact that this friend to whom she could pour out her heart as to no other person would be left behind when she went back to the city? She did not know. But even with the pain there, she felt peace. It could all be left safely with the Lord.

Steve came out and they turned back toward the farm. They felt the peace and quiet of the night about them, and Steve drove slowly as if to prolong the trip. After some time he spoke.

"And what now? Back to the city?"

"Not for a time. Mother will need me. Taking care of an invalid isn't easy under any conditions. Mother is very tired, Jim says, so I must stay to pump water, carry coal and clean lamp chimneys for weeks yet—maybe months. If I can be spared before October I may ask Dot's folks to take me in. But I actually want to stay a while. Having struggled through a hard winter in the old house, I'd like to see spring and summer. I want to see the apple orchard and the lilacs in bloom. Allie May used to tell us how beautiful they were, but it was always summer by the time we could come."

"Haven't grown fond of the old house with all its inconveniences, have you?"

"Yes, I have. That is one of the strangest things about it. The night that I decided we'd have to come here I was almost ill of frustration and rebellion. Now it seems more like home than the place in the city. It has been a battlefield, but I won some notable victories. I wish Dad and Allie May would decide to keep the old place. But that would be silly, I guess. Dad can't manage it and neither Jim nor Kurt is interested in it. Allie May has her own place elsewhere. I wish I were a man. I'd buy it and farm it myself! But I'm not, so I presume it will be sold if we can find a buyer who wants such an old place."

"I have one ready to take it over in October if your father approves. I think he will, because he told me that was what he wanted to do. And I asked Sherry about it after supper and she gave me her O.K. So we may consider it sold."

"I'm sorry," she said, with a break in her voice, "but life is like that. I won't grieve, because I promised my Lord I'd trust Him to lead, and if He leads away from here He will lead into other places of blessing."

"And now Steve Barrett has to quit fooling around and start to make his living in earnest. I've just been cleaning up my dad's affairs so far. The Martin estate was the last big one."

"What are you going to do? You won't go away, will you? I can't think of you anywhere else. You seem to belong here."

"Well, here I stay. I'm to be attorney for the bank at Sparta and also for the canning factory there. I'll live here and drive over every day. It's only eight miles. If the roads get too bad, I can take the train. I like it better here, and I don't want to go so far from Aunt Molly. She isn't young any more and she needs someone to look after her. It's a small-town job, but I'm a small-town man and I like it."

"It's rather wonderful to let the Lord lead, and then just rest in His leading. Even when we forget, He keeps on guiding and guarding."

"It *is* wonderful. We don't have to know the why of His leading either, though often He gives us a glimpse of His purposes to reassure us."

"That reminds me of what happened tonight while we were doing dishes. Aunt Molly said suddenly, 'Oh, why didn't I mention that post office before Allie May when it happened? I talked to ever'one else about it. It woulda saved such a lot of sorrowin'.' Quick as a flash Sherry answered. 'Don't ever have any regrets, Aunt Mauwy. I have left mine all behind. The way was hard but it led to Don and I'm not going to be sorry. Mother and Daddy and my grandfathers all see now why it had to happen, and I can trust. Don and I are together and I've found his Saviour. His parents love me and I love them. We're going on and not looking back.' Isn't she a dear to look at it that way?"

"She's so happy that the past will never bother her again. You know, Ginny, I decided last night after I went home that seeing a new soul born into the kingdom was the greatest joy on earth. I'm ashamed not to have tried harder to win souls for the Lord."

"I hadn't been interested in such work either. I can think now of so many chances I've missed."

"So can I. But you've been a good witness this year. I've been a Christian ever since I was twelve, but during my college years I wandered pretty far from the standards that Aunt Molly set. Last summer I had a deeper experience and I've been growing since then. But I was lonely for some other young person to whom I could talk about it. Then you came. Your unselfishness and your patience and your determination to do your work whether you like it or not were a big inspiration to me. And your *desperate* desire to win Sherry made me realize that it was *my* job also."

"When I was first saved, when I was ten, I was so happy that I thought the whole world must see it in my face. I was sure that I would never again be sad or unhappy about anything. I found out all too soon, however, that life isn't all mountaintop glory."

"No, not even the Christian life. It's falling and rising and falling again because we won't let the Lord do the leading. And it's 'fighting and fears, within, without.' But we don't have to fight alone, and we need not fear if He leads."

They rode in silence then, each busy with thoughts of all the things that had happened since they met last October. Steve spoke first.

"The man who wants to buy the farm plans to make some changes. He can't do a great deal, for he isn't wealthy, but he wants to make it comfortable. Having lived in it for six months, you should have some ideas that would help him. Want to pass them on?"

"Put in a furnace," she said promptly.

"Poor little fireman!" he said, with a laugh. "It's been pretty tough, hasn't it?"

"Well—a furnace would have helped. Next after that, some plumbing. With that deep well and the big cistern there's plenty of water, and an electric pump could bring it into the house."

"So you'd have electricity, too?"

"It would be foolish not to have it with that high-line going right down the road by us, wouldn't it?"

"Yes, indeed. Well, those things are already planned, Haven't you any extra ideas—some clever changes you'd like to make that only a woman would think of?"

"Well—smooth the lane and gravel it so that one wouldn't get stuck in muddy weather. That's obvious, too, I suppose. No owner would drive over that lane very many times without planning to fix it better. I wonder why Grandpa didn't keep it in better condition."

"He did. But he wasn't road-minded as this generation is. To him a good road was one that could be traveled in a buggy or his old car at a pace that a man could run."

"There's only one other thing I'd change. If it were my place, I'd like to leave it as it is so far as that would be consistent with efficient living in this age. The one change I would make would be to let in a little more light. There were times this winter, even on sunny days, when I wanted to push out a wall! So—I'd take out the two front windows in the parlor and put in one big one. And I woundn't smother it in drapes or hangings either. I'd sit there in the winter and look out over the village and all the valley."

"I thought a woman could see what was really needed. I wouldn't have thought of that in fifty years! But I'm bright enough to appreciate it when you produce the idea. It shall be done."

"Can you make the plans for the new owner?"

Steve did not answer at once, but watched the road carefully until they came to a lane that Virginia knew led only to the old Ormand house, which was as dark as if its occupants were asleep. Turning down it, he drew off to the side and stopped the car. Virginia spoke anxiously.

"What's the matter? Is anything wrong with the car?"

"Not a thing. We're getting too close to home to suit me. I want to talk some more and I don't want to go inside. I like the outside and the dark better. If we stopped in your lane, Aunt Molly or Sherry would hear the car and would come out to investigate why we weren't coming in. I don't want them around. In other words, I'm setting the stage for a proposal."

"Oh!"

"Hadn't you suspected what I was leading up to?"

"No—er—what do you mean?"

"Hadn't you any idea that I was the man who planned to buy the farm?"

"*You?* The farm? You mean you—"

"Sure, I mean me! I have talked to both Jim and Sherry about it. Sherry approves one hundred per cent and Jim is sure it will be O.K. with your dad, especially if you will take over the job of the farmer's wife."

She looked up at him, wondering if she should take him seriously. It was not like Steve to joke, but he had been so casual in his relationship with her that she had never thought of him as having any feeling for her other than that of a friend. In the dim light she could not see his face clearly enough for it to reveal the answer to her indecision. Steve must have realized this, for he put his arm around her shoulders and drew her close to his side.

"Wake up, Ginny dear! I'm not joking. As soon as your Dad is able, we'll sign the papers. I'm asking you here and now if you'll marry me—not because I need a housekeeper, nor because the old place needs a mistress, but just because I love you. Even before I saw you, when Jim wrote me what you had planned to do, I thought you must be something pretty special in the way of womanhood. All winter I've watched you and I've come to love you so much that I can't think of the possibility of your not returning that love.

I wanted to tell you about it long ago, but everything was in such a tangle that it seemed selfish to be thinking of my affairs. But God has touched all the tangled strings and they're straight, so the way is clear. You do love me, don't you, Ginny?"

Her hand reached for his, and she clasped it tightly without speaking. He waited while his words became meaningful to her.

So this was the plan the Master Builder had in mind when He pushed over her block-house of self-will! This way was a better way, a happier way, than that of her own choice. She knew without a doubt that she loved Steve Barrett as she never could have loved another, knew that with him she could face a life of happy service for the Master they loved, knew that together they could serve in His vineyard and bring forth for Him fruit for tomorrow—fruit that should abound more and more to the glory of the Master.

Then she turned to him and, drawing his face down to her own, said unsteadily, "I love you so much Steve, that I can't tell you how much! But I'll be a farmer's wife or a lawyer's wife—or—or anything God says. I can't tell you what —oh, Steve!"

Steve apparently did not want her to try, for his kiss effectually sealed her lips.

THE ZONDERVAN PAPERBACK SERIES
Each 95¢

THE REBELLIOUS PLANET — Lon Woodrum   No. 12292s

YOU CAN WITNESS WITH CONFIDENCE —
Rosalind Rinker   No. 10714s

THE GOSPEL BLIMP — Joe Bayly   No. 12288p

FIND FREEDOM — Billy Graham   No. 9716s

THE YEARS THAT COUNT — Rosalind Rinker   No. 10715s

PLAY BALL! — James Hefley   No. 9797s

PRAYER—CONVERSING WITH GOD—Rosalind Rinker   No. 10716p

LIFE IS FOR LIVING — Betty Carlson   No. 9384s

SCIENCE RETURNS TO GOD — James H. Jauncey   No. 9927s

NEVER A DULL MOMENT — Eugenia Price   No. 10584s

SO YOU'RE A TEENAGE GIRL — Jill Renich   No. 10706s

ABOVE OURSELVES — James H. Jauncey   No. 9950s

BECOMING A CHRISTIAN — Rosalind Rinker   No. 10718s

BUT GOD! — V. Raymond Edman   No. 9555s

FIND OUT FOR YOURSELF — Eugenia Price   No. 10603s

THE SAVING LIFE OF CHRIST — W. Ian Thomas   No. 10908s

YOUR CHILD — Anna B. Mow   No. 12256s

SAY 'YES' TO LIFE — Anna B. Mow   No. 10383s

KNOWING GOD'S SECRETS — John Hunter   No. 9883s

THEY FOUND THE SECRET — V. Raymond Edman   No. 9564s

WE'RE NEVER ALONE — Eileen Guder   No. 9710s

MAN TO MAN — Richard C. Halverson   No. 6818s

A WOMAN'S WORLD — Clyde M. Narramore   No. 12230p

LIFE AND LOVE — Clyde M. Narramore   No. 10412p

YOUNG ONLY ONCE — Clyde M. Narramore   No. 10414s

LIMITING GOD — John Hunter   No. 9884s

GAMES FOR ALL OCCASIONS—Carlson and Anderson   No. 9051p

WOMAN TO WOMAN — Eugenia Price   No. 10589p

PILGRIM'S PROGRESS — John Bunyan   No. 6610s

BILLY GRAHAM — John Pollock   No. 10571p

5500 QUESTIONS AND ANSWERS ON THE WHOLE
   BIBLE   No. 9624p